Albert Whitman & Company
Chicago, Illinois

For Chrissie, Alex, and Josie

Library of Congress Cataloging-in-Publication Data

Edge, Christopher.
Twelve minutes to midnight / Christopher Edge ; illustrations by Eric Orchard.
pages cm
ISBN 978-0-8075-8133-9
[1. Mystery and detective stories. 2. Supernatural—Fiction. 3. Psychiatric hospitals—Fiction. 4. Publishers and publishing—Fiction. 5. Authorship—Fiction. 6. Orphans—Fiction. 7. London (England)—History—19th century—Fiction. 8. Great Britain—History—Victoria, 1837–1901—Fiction.] I. Orchard, Eric, illustrator. II. Title.
PZ7.E2265Tw 2014
[Fic]—dc23 2013029481

First published in the UK in 2012 by Nosy Crow Ltd.
Published in 2014 by Albert Whitman & Company

Printed in the United States of America.
10 9 8 7 6 5 4 3 2 1 LB 18 17 16 15 14 13
4/2014

For more information about Albert Whitman & Company,
visit our web site at www.albertwhitman.com.

I

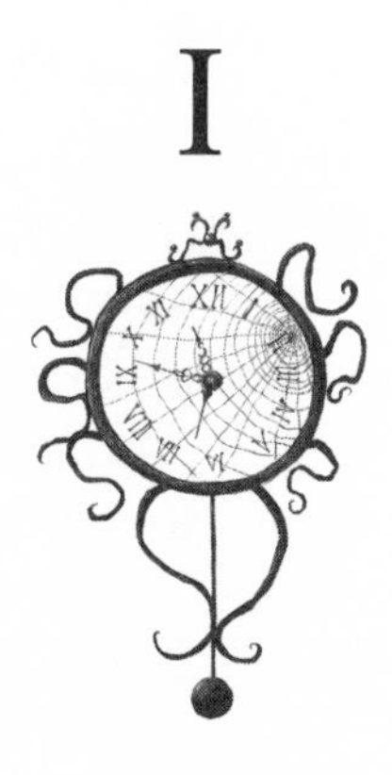

Montgomery Flinch gripped the sides of the reading lectern, his knuckles whitening as he stared out into the darkness of the auditorium. His bristling eyebrows arched and the gleam of his dark eyes seemed to dart across the faces of each audience member in turn. A mesmerized silence hung over the stage as if the theatre itself were holding its breath as it waited for the conclusion to his latest spine-chilling tale. The expectant hush seemed to deepen as Flinch finally began to speak.

"And when he turned and looked into the mirror, his trembling visage a cracked alabaster in the moonlight, he saw the dread face of Dr. Cameron staring back at him, the man that he had murdered some seven years before."

The dimmed gaslights lining the walls of the theatre flickered faintly as a shocked gasp rippled through the audience.

Flinch's face twisted into a grotesque grimace,

his voice now a guttural rasp that echoed around the auditorium.

"'I'm back,' the face in the mirror snarled. The man shrank in fear as Cameron's gnarled fingers reached through the glass. Stumbling backward, he dashed the lamp from the table, darkness shrouding the violent scene as the two men struggled, until only one figure was left standing."

Montgomery Flinch paused, his dark hooded eyes looking up from the last page of the manuscript stacked on the lectern in front of him. A low whimper was audible from the back of the stalls as the audience shivered in their seats. Flinch began to read again, his voice trembling slightly as though fearful of what it was about to reveal.

"Reaching out, a wizened hand righted the lamp and, as its warm pool of light spilled across the room, the hunched form of Dr. Cameron stepped toward the ornate mirror. Imprisoned there behind the glass, his murderer raised his hands in a desperate plea of pity.

"'I'm sorry,' he cried, the ghosts of his words whispering behind the glass. 'Please, I beg of you—'

"With a hiss of satisfaction, Dr. Cameron raised his stout walking stick high, its brass-tipped ferrule glinting in the lamplight, and with an unnatural strength far beyond the capabilities of his frail form, he brought the cane crashing down with a whip crack."

Flinch brought his palm down on the lectern with a thunderous report.

"The mirror shattered into a thousand pieces, and, for a moment, in every single shard, the face of the last Earl of Pomeroy could be glimpsed, his mouth stretched in an endless scream as his dark and murderous deeds were finally avenged."

In the front row, three young women fainted dead away, their consorts frantically ransacking the previously unexplored hinterlands of beaded purses in search of smelling salts to revive their swooning spouses. Farther back in the stalls, an elderly gentleman in a navy-blue frock coat clutched at his chest, his drink-mottled cheeks wheezing as a paroxysm of fear overwhelmed him. But around them, the audience rose to its feet as one, thunderous applause filling the auditorium as Montgomery Flinch bowed deeply.

The evening was a resounding success. This rare appearance by the reclusive Master of the Macabre and sneak preview of his latest story would have hordes of eager readers queuing in the streets tomorrow for its exclusive appearance in the pages of the *Penny Dreadful.* And to think, nobody had even heard of the name Montgomery Flinch a mere twelve months before when the *Penny Dreadful* was a fourth-rate magazine scraping by with a readership counted in the dozens. Now, ever since the appearance of Montgomery Flinch's fictions in its pages, the *Penny Dreadful* had a circulation close to half a million, the magazine flying off the bookstands every month as the readers devoured Flinch's dread tales. In the fading days of the nineteenth century, the fame of the man himself even threatened to eclipse that of Dickens, Kipling, and Doyle—the literary world astounded by his meteoric rise to stardom.

As Montgomery Flinch stood there in the spotlight, his hands raised in false modesty as he soaked up the applause, the pinched face of the theatre manager nervously peered around the crimson drapes at the side of the stage. With a shuffling gait, the black-suited impresario inched his way across the stage as the house lights were raised until finally he was standing by the author's side, the ovation still ringing out across the theatre. He nodded toward Flinch with an obsequious bow and then, turning back to the audience, held out his hands to gesture for silence.

Reluctantly, the applause faded away into a smattering of handclaps, the theatregoers returning to their seats as the manager began to speak.

"May I once again extend the heartfelt thanks of the Lyceum Theatre to the illustrious Montgomery Flinch for finally breaking his silence and sharing this exclusive performance of his Christmas tale of terror with us," he fawned. "This story will be published tomorrow in the December issue of the *Penny Dreadful*, available from all good booksellers."

Another round of applause broke over the stage again, the audience sharing their thanks in the only way they knew how.

Reaching inside his frock coat, the theatre manager pulled out his pocket watch and glanced down at its face, nervously twisting its chain with his other hand.

"And as the performance appears to have finished slightly ahead of schedule," he continued, "I'd like to throw open the stage to any questions from the audience. I'm sure Mr. Flinch would welcome this unique opportunity to talk directly with the devotees of his most remarkable fictions."

The impresario turned back toward Montgomery Flinch, whose face had cracked in horror. Flinch drew back from the lectern, his dark eyes flashing with fear.

"I really don't know if I can—"

A forest of hands reached up from every corner of the theatre. Questions fired toward the stage in an excited hubbub of voices.

"Mr. Flinch! Why are your stories so scary?"

"Where do you get your ideas from?"

"Monty! What's your next story going to be about?"

"Ladies and gentlemen," the theatre manager struggled to make his voice heard above the sudden din, "one at a time, please."

From the middle of the front row, a man's

booming voice hushed the crowd as his question rang out as clear as a bell.

"What's the big secret, Flinch?"

There was a sharp intake of breath as the audience craned to see the face of the questioner. The voice belonged to a tall, thin man in a pinstriped suit who leaned forward in his seat toward the light spilling off the stage. His neatly trimmed moustache gave his lean, pockmarked face the appearance of someone trying to look older than their meager years. In his hand, he held an open notebook, pen poised above the paper as he waited for Montgomery Flinch's reply.

The author's broad shoulders sagged as he reached forward and grasped hold of the lectern's edge.

"Wh-wh-what do you mean?" he stuttered, his face suddenly pale beneath the spotlight. A single bead of sweat slicked down his forehead and poised suspended from the end of his long nose before falling silently onto the manuscript pages below.

"You're the most celebrated author in Britain, but nobody knows the first thing about you," the young journalist continued, his voice echoing around the now hushed theatre. "Other authors toil for years in obscurity, but here you are, an overnight star." His eyes glittered mischievously. "I'll ask you again, what exactly is your secret?"

"There's no secret," Flinch blustered, waving

his hands dismissively at the question. "I'm just lucky I suppose..."

The journalist frowned, his eyes narrowing as he opened his mouth to speak again, but before the words could escape his lips, a shrill cry echoed across the theatre.

"That's not true!"

The eyes of the audience swiveled to the far end of the front row. There, a young girl in a fashionable red dress had risen to her feet, her outstretched finger pointing straight at the stage. Her long dark hair was pulled back from her face and her pretty green eyes sparkled with indignation.

"I've read every single one of your stories, Mr. Flinch," she said, her voice rising in protest. "It isn't luck that has made your name, but sheer dazzling talent. Nobody else could have dreamed up such nightmarish visions, created such mesmerizing characters or crafted your spine-chilling tales. We don't need to know your secret—just give thanks that you are willing to share your stories with us."

Still standing in the spotlight, Montgomery Flinch's face flushed with relief. Reaching into his pocket for a handkerchief, he dabbed at his brow as yet another peal of applause rang out from the audience to acclaim the young girl's words. In the front row, the journalist was still struggling to make himself heard. He glared at the girl, a gleam of recognition in his gaze, but his voice was lost in the tumultuous ovation.

"That's very kind of you to say," Flinch finally replied as the applause gradually dimmed. "And now I really must bid you all good night, but I'd be most honored, Miss, if you could join me backstage so that I can present you with a signed copy of my latest tale."

Stepping out from behind the lectern, he held out his right hand toward the girl and the audience's applause redoubled at this unexpected act of kindness. The dark-haired girl slowly climbed the steps at the front of the stage until finally she was standing in front of the author. Then, with a final bow to the audience, the two of them exited stage left, disappearing behind the heavy crimson drapes.

As stamps and cheers shook the stage, the author led the way through the maze of corridors backstage. His broad frame brushed past discarded pieces of painted scenery and forgotten props, clothes rails filled with musty costumes, the smell of greasepaint heavy in the air. The two of them walked in silence until they reached the dressing rooms, stopping outside a door with a fading star nailed to the peeling green paint. Montgomery Flinch unlocked his dressing room and ushered the girl inside.

The poky room was dominated by a large mirror surrounded by lights. This sat on a solitary table overflowing with vases of flowers, empty glasses, and crumpled sheets of paper. Around the room, more brightly colored costumes hung from rails amid the decapitated bodies of mannequins, ghostly relics of the actors who had gone before.

With a heavy sigh, Montgomery Flinch slumped into the chair in front of his dressing-room table. He reached toward a crystal decanter filled with a dark amber liquid and, with a shaking hand, poured a generous measure into the nearest empty glass.

Closing the door behind her, the dark-haired girl turned toward the author, her pale face now wreathed in fury.

"What in the blazes do you think you are doing?"

II

"I hired you to give a reading of Montgomery Flinch's latest story, not to start answering questions from every Tom, Dick, and Harry in the theatre!"

The girl's emerald eyes blazed angrily as she jabbed her finger at the author, who cowered in his chair, gulping his drink down greedily as though he hoped he could disappear into the bottom of the glass.

"And why on earth did you say that your success was down to luck? This is the very first glimpse the world has of the legendary Montgomery Flinch, a man shrouded in mystery whose every printed word is dissected by the critics, and you make him sound like some Grub Street hack!"

"But, Penelope," the man interrupted, "that pinstriped fiend with the notebook, I thought he knew—"

"He knows nothing," the girl snapped. She

drew herself up as tall as her thirteen years would allow. "That journalist has been sniffing around the offices of the *Penny Dreadful* for weeks now, trying to wheedle an interview with the elusive Montgomery Flinch, but I've always managed to keep him at bay. That's the reason I hired you, Mr. Maples, to give a carefully stage-managed appearance from Montgomery Flinch to promote the Christmas edition of the *Penny Dreadful*, keep the reading public happy, and get the press off our backs."

Penelope shook her head as she watched the actor refill his glass, the crystal decanter now half empty.

"If I hadn't jumped in when I did, Lord knows what you'd have said next. Your résumé stated that you were the finest actor not currently employed on the London stage, an extraordinary performer who can bring a whole cast of characters alive." She fished a tattered piece of paper out of her purse. "And I quote, 'With his superb command of the stage, Monty Maples gives you an entire theatrical company under one hat.'" The young girl snapped her purse shut with a frown. "But if the chaotic end to tonight's performance is anything to go by, I may have to rethink our arrangement."

Monty Maples seemed to shrink in his chair like a scolded puppy.

"You didn't like my performance?"

Penelope pursed her lips, the fire that had blazed in her eyes since she'd entered the dressing room slowly fading as she met the actor's gaze. Monty's eyes blinked owlishly as if he was about to cry.

"I didn't say I didn't like your performance," she replied, her voice softening. "It's just that when you go off script like that...We need to improvise more—make sure you're ready for every eventuality. It's important that nobody has any doubt that you really are Montgomery Flinch."

Monty took another sip from his glass, lowering his gaze beneath his bristling eyebrows, but a trace of self-pity lingered in his eyes.

"The reading of the story itself," Penelope continued, "that was rather good."

The actor sprang forward in his chair, dregs of amber liquid spilling from his glass.

"Did you see how I had them in the palm of my hand?" he declared, his face gripped by passion as his voice boomed out with the same force as it had on the stage. "Did you hear the squeals when I described how he dragged the doctor's body into the depths of the moor, the blood falling from his fingers like flakes of crimson snow?"

Penelope nodded, a small smile creeping across her lips. "I knew that scene would get them when I wrote it," she admitted.

"Oh, and it did," Monty proclaimed, beaming magnanimously. "And what an ending, I swear I could hear the tread of a mouse as the audience waited for me to read the very last lines."

Penelope blushed, a crimson stain creeping up her cheeks.

"They did seem to like it, didn't they?"

"Like it?" Monty boomed. "They were absolutely petrified! Why I've never known such a reaction since my performance of the Scottish—"

A knock at the dressing-room door cut Monty's sentence short. The two of them looked at each other, a momentary flash of panic passing in front of their eyes. There was a second loud knock, followed by two quieter raps, and then the final thud of a fist against the door.

Penelope's slender shoulders sagged with relief and she quickly turned to open the door. Outside, a tall, silver-haired man dressed in a gray worsted twill coat stood waiting with his top hat carried under his arm. He peered down at her with a hawkish stare.

"Miss Tredwell." The elderly man gave a curt nod as he stepped into the cramped dressing room. "Mr. Maples."

Monty quickly straightened in his seat, pushing his now empty glass behind a vase of flowers on his dressing-room table. Behind the silver-haired gentleman a scruffy-looking boy staggered into the room, his white shirt splattered with a web of ink stains. He carried a stack of what looked like large paperback books, which he spilled onto the dressing-room table before turning to Penelope with a broad grin.

"Here you are, Penny—hot off the presses!"

"Thanks, Alfie," Penelope replied with a smile as she stepped forward to inspect the latest edition of the *Penny Dreadful.*

Alfie pulled off his cap to reveal a tousled mop of blond hair and turned to Monty, who was now perched pensively in his chair.

"And your performance tonight, Mr. Maples..." He whistled. "What a show-stopper! I thought some of those old dears in there were going to keel right over when you read the part where the doctor was pushed into the cider press."

Monty's reddening face broke into a relieved smile.

"Why, thank you, dear boy," he replied graciously. He flicked his hair from his face, the self-conscious gesture reflected in the brightly lit mirror. "It was like capturing lightning in a bottle. I knew that if I could just convey the power of Flinch's words then—"

"Ah, yes," the bloodless tones of the silver-haired man cut across Monty's self-regarding bluster, "if we could first discuss your performance tonight, Mr. Maples?"

Monty glanced up fearfully, the smile quickly fading from his face.

"I don't believe that Miss Tredwell's unscheduled appearance onstage tonight was at all to our benefit," the man continued, his forehead creasing so that his face resembled that of a benevolent troll. "In fact, as her lawyer and guardian, I would assert that the farther she stays away from the limelight, the less likely the chances of Montgomery Flinch's real identity ever being unmasked."

"Don't worry, William." Penelope placed her hand on her guardian's arm. "Monty and I have discussed things. Teething problems aside, this was a good start to Montgomery Flinch's life in the public gaze."

Monty nodded eagerly.

"I will polish my lines, Mr. Wigram," he reassured the man. "Practice countless improvisations. Montgomery Flinch may be the most challenging role of my career, but I assure you I'll give my finest ever performance." He met the gaze of the silver-haired man, who was still looking at him askance. "But if I could just trouble you now for my fee."

The lawyer's frown deepened for a moment, then he reached into the inside pocket of his jacket and drew out a crisp white envelope. He placed the envelope in Monty's outstretched hand. The actor eagerly tore it open and then blew out his cheeks as he read the figure written on the check.

"That will do nicely," he said, placing the check inside his own jacket and then tapping the pocket with a smile.

"Remember," Mr. Wigram cautioned, "this is an opening installment. As you continue to discharge your duties in the role of Montgomery Flinch, further payments will be made."

"A toast!" Monty cried with delight as he turned back to his dressing-room table, reaching again for the decanter. "To the continued success of Montgomery Flinch."

Penelope reached out with swift fingers and spirited the bottle away before Monty could pour another drop in his glass.

"I think that success will be best assured if you go easy on the toasts," she reminded him with a stern stare.

Chastened, Monty nodded his head with an apologetic mumble. Behind him, Alfie failed to hide the smirk on his face as he took a sip from one of Monty's discarded glasses before grimacing in sudden disgust.

Penelope turned back to her guardian.

"Is everything well at the office?" she asked.

After the *Penny Dreadful* had been bequeathed to her by her late father, following his sad passing alongside her mother in the North-West Frontier Uprising in British India, Penelope had single-handedly acted as the magazine's editor, lead author, and publisher, hiding her true identity behind countless pseudonyms.

"Everything is fine," Wigram nodded in reply. "The final galley proofs were signed off by the printer this afternoon. By tomorrow morning, every bookshop and newsstand in London will have the latest edition of the *Penny Dreadful* on display, and by early tomorrow evening, it will have reached the provinces. The sales forecasts are very strong, especially now that Montgomery Flinch is promoting his work."

The lawyer reached again into his jacket pocket, a new frown creasing his forehead.

"There was one item of correspondence that arrived today that I thought you should see, though. A most unusual letter addressed to Montgomery Flinch from one of his many devoted readers."

Penelope sighed. Ever since Flinch's tales of supernatural terror had started appearing in the pages of the *Penny Dreadful*, a cavalcade of cranks, crackpots, and charlatans had filled her letter box with outlandish letters and telegrams. Just because Montgomery Flinch's stories told of strange and preternatural happenings beyond the mortal knowledge of man, these letter writers believed that Montgomery Flinch could help them to solve the unearthly mysteries that afflicted them.

She took the letter from her guardian's hand with a weary shake of her head. This would be from yet another half-crazed reader who thought that Flinch could swoop down like Doyle's Sherlock Holmes and solve whatever unfathomable enigma was contained within the envelope. The postmark showed it had been sent from St. George's Fields the previous evening, but as she slipped the embossed paper from the already open envelope, she was surprised to see the official crest of the Bethlem Royal Hospital on the letterhead.

Bethlem, or Bedlam as it was better known on the streets of the city, was the notorious lunatic asylum which housed London's mad; the ramshackle hospital south of the Thames overflowing with the tragic human waste of those who had lost their minds. As she began to read, Penelope raised her eyebrows in bewilderment. Perhaps some of Flinch's readers weren't half-crazed at all.

Dear Mr. Flinch,

I am writing to you as I do not know where else I can turn. The Governors of the hospital would be alarmed beyond belief to learn that I had contacted you, but the sinister events of the past six months defy conventional medical thinking and, though I fear to say it, convince me that some supernatural hand is at work on these wards. I have tried every conceivable remedy, sought help from many learned men, but to no avail. As an avid reader of your stories, I am convinced that you alone have the eldritch knowledge that will be able to cast a light into the darkness that has fallen over the Royal Bethlem Hospital. I would value your assistance and pray that you come as soon as is possible.

Yours faithfully,
Dr. Charles Morris, M.D., F.R.C.P.
Physician Superintendent, Royal Bethlem Hospital

As Penelope finished reading the letter, her fingers twitched. The beginning of a story started to take shape in her mind. This letter held the promise of a mystery, an astounding tale for Montgomery Flinch to craft. A gothic horror set amid the barred cells of Bedlam, its corridors echoing with ghostly wails; the perfect story for the next issue of the *Penny Dreadful*. And here was the very excuse she needed to see the place for herself. An excited smile slowly spread across her face.

Unaware of this development, Monty rose from his chair. He grabbed his top hat and coat from where they were draped across a mannequin and he turned toward the dressing-room door.

"My friends, I must bid you farewell," he said, raising his hat with a valedictory wave. "The evening is still young and I can hear the sound of my club calling."

"Not so fast, Monty."

Penelope's voice stopped the actor in his tracks.

"I'm afraid your evening's work isn't yet

complete," she said with an apologetic grin. "Montgomery Flinch and I have an urgent appointment tonight at Bedlam."

III

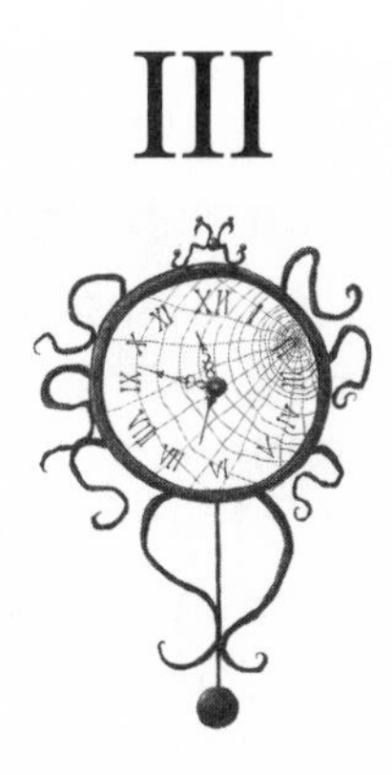

"I don't know why you had to drag me here," Monty hissed, shivering in his rain-splattered coat as he stood waiting with Penelope outside the physician superintendent's office. The shadows thrown by the wall lamps danced across the actor's worried face.

Penelope shook her head.

"Dr. Morris is expecting to meet Montgomery Flinch himself—the only man who can unravel whatever strange story is unfolding here. Now stick to the script and remember what we agreed," she replied in a hurried whisper.

They had arrived at Bedlam just after 11 p.m., the hospital suddenly looming in front of them out of the fog and drizzle. Above the entrance, its high dome and six-columned portico were wreathed in pale shrouds of mist, while the wings of the hospital stretched out on either side, countless rows of pitch-black windows staring out into the night like empty eyes. As they left their hansom cab and scurried inside the hospital, Penelope thought she could almost hear the low moans of the patients incarcerated there, carried on the chill wind that whipped across St. George's Fields.

When the orderly manning the entrance had heard the name Montgomery Flinch, he scuttled away to rouse Dr. Morris, although not before pulling out a well-worn copy of the *Penny Dreadful* from under his desk and proffering it to Monty with a pen for him to sign. Raising an eyebrow, Monty had scrawled the name *Montgomery Flinch* across the magazine's cover. The young orderly had gasped in excitement and disappeared into the depths of the hospital clutching his literary prize. Now Penelope and Monty stood awaiting the physician's arrival.

"Mr. Flinch!"

The office door swung open to reveal a small, stout man of about fifty years, thinning strands of pale white hair pulled across his balding head. Two restless gray eyes gleamed brightly behind gold-rimmed glasses as the doctor stepped forward to seize Monty's hand.

"You came," Dr. Morris cried, shaking Monty's hand in gratitude as though he was afraid to let him go. His clothes were disheveled as if he had slept in them, and his round plump face was seamed with lines of trouble. "When I sent you the letter, I didn't dare to hope..."

"I must admit I found your letter intriguing, Dr.

Morris," Monty replied, his commanding tone meant to soothe as he sought to extricate his hand from the doctor's grasp, "although somewhat mysterious. What exactly are these sinister events to which you refer?"

"The madness," the doctor replied, his voice dropping to a dolorous whisper, "it's spreading."

His eyes darted past Monty and, for the first time, caught sight of Penelope standing patiently behind the actor's broad frame. He shrank back toward his office with a yelp of alarm.

"Mr. Flinch, I expected you to come alone," Dr. Morris cried, "not bring a child! This matter is really not suitable for a young girl's sensibilities."

Monty brushed the doctor's protest away with a wave of his hand.

"Dr. Morris, this is my niece, Miss Penelope Tredwell," he replied. "She has read every single story that I have written and never once fainted in a swoon or turned a hair at even my most gruesome scene. She has an enlightened mind and a strong constitution and I absolutely insist that she stays by my side if I am to help you with this matter."

The doctor stood frozen, his face aghast at the thought of a mere child learning the sinister secret he was hiding. With a reluctant nod, he stepped forward again and shook Penelope's hand. His sausage-like fingers were cold and clammy against her skin. Then he quickly ushered the two of them into his office and closed the door behind them.

As the doctor scurried behind his desk, its ornate lamp throwing out a dim circle of light, Penelope quickly glanced about the room. The walls were lined with high bookcases filled with leather-bound volumes—medical textbooks, annual reports, ledgers, and accounts—and as she sank into the stiff-backed chair next to Monty, the two of them facing the doctor across his desk, she saw with a faint tingle of satisfaction, the collected volumes of the *Penny Dreadful* taking pride of place on the bookshelf directly behind the doctor's balding head.

"So, Dr. Morris," Monty began as he settled into his chair, "what do you mean when you say the madness is spreading? This *is* an asylum, isn't it? I would have thought that was an occupational hazard?"

The doctor's eyebrows furrowed, but if he recognized the barb in Monty's question he didn't show it.

"The Royal Bethlem Hospital understands and can treat the many forms of conventional madness," Dr. Morris replied, the words rolling from his down-turned mouth. "The catatonics, the paranoiacs, the depressives, and the manics—all find a restorative regime in place for them here at the hospital."

Penelope raised a suspicious eyebrow. The

notorious legend of the cruelty of Bedlam with its deranged inmates kept in chains still ran strong. "You mean the leeches and the bleeding?" she asked with a wry smile.

Glancing toward her, Dr. Morris frowned.

"Such outmoded practices ceased decades ago," he replied curtly. "This is a modern hospital. Patients today receive the very latest medical therapies and treatment. Until the recent unsettling events, the recovery rate for our patients was nearing as high as twenty percent."

"What recent events?"

Ignoring Penelope's question, the doctor turned dismissively away before addressing his answer to Monty alone.

"Of late, a dark cloud has fallen over the hospital," he revealed, "a terrible affliction that has every patient in its grasp. This is no ordinary madness. If I wasn't a man of science, Mr. Flinch, I would say it was the work of the Devil himself."

Monty leaned forward in his chair, his hands gripping the armrests as a sticky bead of sweat ran down his forehead.

"Pray continue," he said, a faint tremor evident in his voice, as beside him Penelope silently fumed.

"It started six months ago," the doctor replied. "On a regular ward round late at night in the men's wing, one of our nurses observed a sleeping patient suddenly rise from his bed and, in a catatonic trance, start writing across the wall of his cell. The man wrote for nearly an hour, scribing with a broken piece of chalk as he covered the wall with words, before finally returning to his bed, seemingly unaware of what he had just done.

"At the end of her shift, the nurse made her report, and at first, we just added this to the patient's list of symptoms," the doctor explained. "Yet another condition for us to treat."

He pushed his glasses back up his nose.

"But the very next night, the man rose from his bed again, and this time the patients in the adjoining cells rose with him. Three patients entering the same trancelike condition at almost exactly the same time—twelve minutes to midnight. All three of them wrote with whatever they could find to hand, scribbling frantically across discarded papers, books, even your own magazine, Mr. Flinch."

Dr. Morris fixed Monty with a leaden stare, his gray eyes haunted behind the spectacle glass.

"Since then, this madness has spread through the hospital like wildfire. Each night, starting at twelve minutes to midnight, more and more patients begin to rise from their beds, all succumbing to this insatiable urge to write. And when they wake the next morning, none of them has any memory of their actions."

Penelope's fingers worried at a loose thread on her dress. The events the doctor was describing seemed more incredible than even the most outlandish tale she'd ever coaxed from the pen of Montgomery Flinch.

"We tried removing paper and writing implements from the cells," the doctor continued, wringing his own hands in despair, "but to no avail. The afflicted still woke and wrote with bloodied fingers against the stones of their cells." The doctor's brow glistened with perspiration in the lamplight. "Every day, the patients seem more agitated. Medicine holds no help for them now. Our trusted therapies and treatments no longer have any effect. My only hope, Mr. Flinch, is that your uncanny mind can find the cure for this malady."

Penelope couldn't hold her silence any longer, couldn't stop herself from blurting out the one question that had to be asked.

"What do they write?"

Taken aback by her temerity, Dr. Morris gave Penelope a cold stare over his gold-rimmed glasses.

"The ravings of madmen," he replied briskly. "Delirious imaginings, preposterous visions—no logic or reason in anything that they write at all. Anyway, you can see for yourself." He glanced up at the clock on the wall of his office. Its minute hand pointed to twenty to the hour, as the hour hand neared twelve. "It's nearly time."

Rising from his desk, Dr. Morris gestured for them to follow him. Turning left as they exited his office, the doctor quickly led them toward a gloomy stairwell.

"The basement is where we keep our most troubled patients," he explained, wheezing slightly as he hurried down the single flight of stairs lit with a gas lamp that spluttered as they descended before regaining its yellow glow. "Although, of late, it seems as though the entire hospital is filled with agitation and despair."

At the bottom of the stairwell, Penelope saw a long corridor stretching out in front of them, a dim light suffusing the gloom. The doors of the patient's cells were spaced at regular intervals to the left and to the right, and at the head of the corridor, slumped on a straight-backed chair, an unshaven guard sat dozing, his broad chest slowly rising and falling as Dr. Morris stood crossly in front of him.

The doctor coughed to clear his throat, waking the night orderly from his slumber with a sudden start. The man's bulldog face twisted into a snarl, barely suppressing his rage at being woken. Beneath his left eye, Penelope noticed the broad weal from an old scar slashed across his cheek. Glancing up at the doctor, the disheveled orderly muttered a half-hearted apology as he rose from his chair, a ring of keys clanking around his waist.

"If you could unlock Fitzgerald's cell," Dr. Morris ordered the guard, his frosty tones expressing his displeasure.

Glancing suspiciously at Monty and Penelope as they stood waiting behind the doctor, the night orderly selected a key from his chain and crossed the corridor to a door on his right. Bending his broad shoulders, he unlocked the cell and swung the door open. Dr. Morris gestured for Monty and Penelope to follow him as he stepped inside the cell.

Monty turned to Penelope, a nervous twitch flickering across his fearful face.

"This wasn't what I agreed to," he hissed. "There could be a maniac in there and he expects us to walk right in."

"Pull yourself together," Penelope replied, her voice low and calm. "You're supposed to be Montgomery Flinch, Master of the Macabre, not some lily-livered milksop."

"The cell is currently empty," Dr. Morris's voice floated out into the corridor, "but you'll be able to see the evidence clearly here, Mr. Flinch."

The orderly stood waiting by the cell door, a surly expression fixed to his disfigured face as he watched them both intently. Squaring his shoulders, Monty stepped forward with Penelope close beside him.

As he strode into the cell, Monty held his handkerchief to his face, as though to protect himself from whatever maddening vapors might be lurking there. Next to him, Penelope gasped in amazement as she took in the sight that awaited them.

A single bed, chair, and small table were the only items of furniture in the cell, but its whitewashed walls were covered entirely in words. Scrawled chalk marks, whirls of black ink, even marks made in what looked like blood; an avalanche of language exploding across the walls of the cell. Penelope stepped farther into the room, the single light fixed to the ceiling throwing her shadow across the scene.

"Fitzgerald passed away two nights ago," Dr. Morris revealed. "He was one of the first patients to be afflicted and his mania overwhelmed him in the end. This isn't all that he wrote—there are endless stacks of paper, scraps of his clothing, even carvings on his bedpan—all filled with the same madness that is written across these walls."

Penelope stepped closer, inspecting the wall and trying to decipher the words written there.

...great cities of glass and steel reaching up into the heavens...land mines erupting underfoot in a desolate barbed-wire forest... the mud and the rats and the screams and the dying...sinister iron birds peck at the sky... ruptured metal and the melting of stone...a mushroom cloud rising on the horizon, the smoke devouring an entire city...

Penelope shivered, the unsettling beauty of

the words chilling her blood. She'd expected to read the half-formed rantings of a mind touched by madness, but she sensed some deeper secret was buried beneath these unfathomable words. The strange visions they conjured crept into her mind.

"Quick," the rasp of Dr. Morris's voice interrupted her troubled thoughts, "it's nearly twelve minutes to midnight."

He ushered Monty back out into the corridor, Penelope following close behind. Opening up the shutters of the viewing window into the next cell, the doctor motioned for them to watch. Lifting herself up on her tiptoes, Penelope peered inside. In the darkened room, a patient lay sleeping, his face just visible in the half-light spilling from the window, his body shrouded in a sheet. The doctor glanced down at his pocket watch as the second hand approached the twelve.

"Now," he whispered.

The patient sat bolt upright in his bed, his hands suddenly scrabbling for the paper and pencil left on the table by his bedside. His eyes were still half-shut in some kind of trance, but as his fingers shut around the pencil, he started to write, the words flowing across the paper without a pause. From the cells around them, Penelope could hear the sounds of more patients waking, the thud of their footsteps echoing down the corridor as they rose from their beds, quickly followed by the incessant scratching of pens and the scrape of chalk against stone.

"Mr. Flinch," the doctor turned toward them, his eyes wild with despair, "can you help us?"

Penelope looked up at Monty, the actor's pale face frozen in fear, and then back toward the doctor.

"My uncle will do everything that he can," she replied. "Rest assured of that."

IV

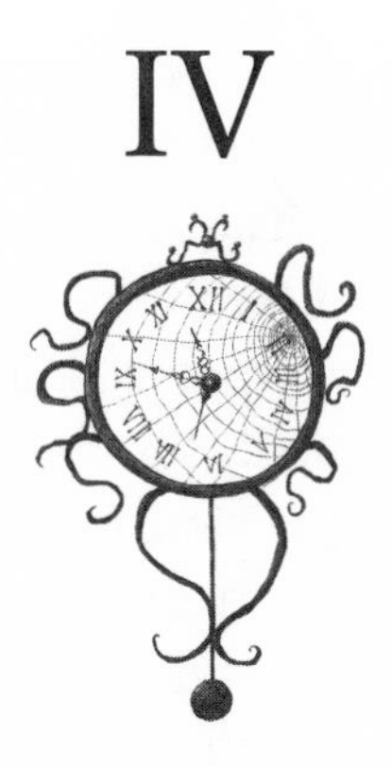

The silent man sat facing Penelope and Monty from across the broad mahogany table, his troubled countenance reflected in the sheen of its polished surface. His eyes were downcast, avoiding their gaze, as his fingers nervously twisted and knotted in a twitching cat's cradle. The same man they had watched hunched over the desk in his cell, his pen *scritch, scritch, scratching* across endless sheets of paper, fewer than twelve hours before.

Rays of watery sunlight peered through the high windows, the frames too small for any patient in search of escape to climb through. The sunlight crept across the faded carpet and shabby furnishings, banishing their melancholy shadows to the edges of the room. In a standing cage in the far corner, a small green bird fluttered anxiously behind its bars.

Back at the table, Penelope slyly dug her elbow into Monty's midriff as the actor sat dozing by her side. With a sharp gasp of surprise, Monty jolted forward, prompted to ask again the questions that had brought them there.

"Ahem." Monty coughed to clear his throat. "Mr. Kemp—what exactly happened at twelve minutes to midnight last night? Why did you wake? What were you writing?"

The man raised his dulled eyes, fixing Monty with a listless stare. He was a thin, sharp-featured man, heading into middle age. His closely cropped hair was peppered with gray, and a half-forgotten sadness lurked in his dark brown eyes. He held Monty's gaze for a moment before dropping his eyes back to the table once more. A maddening silence filled the room.

Monty turned to Penelope, an exasperated frown furrowing his brow.

"It's useless," he hissed out of the corner of his mouth. "I don't know why you had to drag me back here. We've been asking the same questions for the last half hour without any hint of an answer. The man's a vacant fool—he won't tell us anything."

They had arrived back at Bedlam late that morning after a restless night spent holed up in Penelope's guardian's house on the outskirts of the city. As they left again for the hospital, Mr. Wigram had pressed another check into Monty's hand, the second installment of his fee for playing the part of Montgomery Flinch—insurance to make sure he kept to his lines and followed Penelope's every instruction. But now Monty glanced around at the whitewashed walls and barred windows looking as though he'd rather be playing the back end of a pantomime horse.

Penelope shook her head.

"Dr. Morris said that Mr. Kemp was one of the first patients to succumb to the condition. Whatever's happening here, he's been involved from the start. He must know something."

On the other side of the table, Kemp's pale fingers continued to twist and twitch in quickening knots, his hunched body rocking backward and forward. An untidy stack of papers sat on the table between them. As Penelope reached across and picked up the topmost sheet, Kemp flinched at the movement, a naked flicker of fear flashing across his worn face.

Penelope stared down at the litany of words scratched across the page in ink, desperately searching for some kind of meaning among the madness.

Countdown. Ignition. Lift off.
A towering rocket splits the sky, filling the night with fire.
Saturn Five. Apollo Eleven. The Eagle has landed.
One small step for man, one giant leap for mankind.
Collins. Aldrin. Armstrong.

Footprints in moon dust—the stars and stripes flying across a lunar sea.

She shook her head. These were the outlandish imaginings of a mind that had lost its moorings and was floating free into the realms of fantasy. Rockets and eagles. Moon dust and madness. None of it made any sense at all, but some strange power lurked in these words and she was determined to find out what it was.

"What does it mean?" she asked Kemp, the soft tone of her voice low and reassuring. "One small step for man, one giant leap for mankind?"

Kemp's eyes darted nervously to hers, his knuckles whitening as his fingers tightened their grasp.

"Please," Penelope continued, reaching out toward him as her soothing voice tried to coax a response from his lips. "I want to help you."

Kemp shrank back from the table, a wary look drawn across his pale face. He swallowed hard. Then his mouth opened a crack, his tongue flicking nervously across his top lip, before he finally began to speak.

"Every night, I dream such dreams." His voice was a whispery croak, as though he hadn't spoken for an age. "I've seen incredible, impossible things. Rocket ships, star sailors, moon men, and satellites. I've seen this world spinning silently in an endless blackness, held in the palm of one man's hand."

Kemp flung his arm out, gesturing toward the

walls of the drawing room—of the asylum that kept him imprisoned.

"None of this matters. The days of solitude, the doctors, and the drugs. When I sleep, I am free. The world soars beneath my feet and I see such wonders that my heart can barely hold them."

A single tear ran down Kemp's face and fell onto the polished mahogany.

"But why do you write them down?" said Penelope, as next to her, Monty leaned forward to inspect the sheet of paper in her hand.

Kemp's face suddenly darkened. He snatched the sheet out of Penelope's grasp. His arms greedily gathered together the stack of papers remaining on the table and hugged them close to his chest.

"These are my stories," he hissed. "All mine. They come every morning to take them away, but this one isn't finished yet."

"What do you mean?" asked Penelope, taken aback by the man's sudden change in mood. "Who takes them away? And what for?"

Kemp glared at her, his brown eyes filled with suspicion.

"Don't pretend you don't know," he sneered. "You're all in on it; every single one of you. Keeping me locked away here, whilst the world hungers for my genius and the latest tale to fall from my pen. For the *Penny Dreadful*, of course—I am Montgomery Flinch."

Penelope and Monty glanced at each other in

surprise, Kemp's ridiculous words striking them both momentarily silent. It was Monty who spoke again first, a soft chuckle in his voice.

"My dear fellow, you must be mistaken," he told him. "The *Penny Dreadful* publishes only the finest tales of gothic fiction—stories of supernatural horror and suspense. Not scientific romances about moon men and rocket ships. Are you sure you're not Jules Verne or perhaps H. G. Wells? After all," he added pompously, "*I* am Montgomery Flinch."

Sitting next to him, Penelope reached out a hand toward Monty in warning, but it was already too late. Kemp's face crumpled with rage and he flung himself across the table, scattering the papers that fell like snow-white petals to the floor. He grabbed hold of the lapels of Monty's jacket, and pulled his face close to his own.

"You're not Montgomery Flinch," he snarled, spittle flying from his lips.

"Guards! Guards!" Monty's voice cried out in alarm, his face blanched white with fear.

The drawing-room door was flung open as two white-coated orderlies rushed inside. The men pulled Kemp's hands from around Monty's throat and forced the patient down onto the floor. Penelope watched, horrified, as the two men wrapped a long white coat around Kemp to restrain him, the straitjacket pinioning his arms to his sides.

"Thank God," Monty sobbed in relief.

His shaking hands reached up to straighten the disheveled collar on his jacket. Behind him, Kemp howled in despair as the orderlies dragged him backward toward the door.

"Do you have to hurt him?" Penelope pleaded.

One of the burly orderlies glanced back and she saw the scarred face of the guard who had shown them to the cell last night.

"It helps if you don't provoke them, Miss," he replied with a surly sneer. He yanked hard on the straitjacket collar, choking Kemp's cries into silence. "Come on, let's get you back to your cell where you can't disturb the young lady anymore."

The two men bundled Kemp out through the door, his anguished eyes meeting Penelope's gaze for a split second before he was gone.

"That's it," said Monty, his voice trembling as he turned toward Penelope. "We've got to get out of this dreadful place right away. It's not safe. That madman could have killed me—murdered the both of us. If those guards hadn't been there outside..." His sentence stumbled into silence as he glared indignantly at Penelope. "Are you even listening to me?"

Penelope didn't acknowledge Monty's question. She stared down at the papers strewn across the floor, the scattered words making no more sense than when she had first read them. Kemp said that he had dreamed them; every night, at the same time, these fantastical visions. Was that what was happening here? A hospital filled with dreamers?

But Kemp was insane. His delusions of literary grandeur proved that beyond doubt: his outlandish claims that his stories were destined for the pages of the *Penny Dreadful*—that he was Montgomery Flinch himself...

"Penelope!"

Penelope shivered as she glanced up at Monty, the snap of his voice jolting her out of her reverie. Montgomery Flinch didn't exist.

"Did you hear what I said?" Monty asked, a flushed glow slowly returning to his cheeks. "We need to leave right now."

Penelope shook her head. "There's something happening here—something that we're missing." She bent down to gather up the scattered papers. "If these are just dreams, then where are they coming from? What's causing them?"

Her eyes skimmed over the loops and whirls of Kemp's scrawled handwriting that filled the sheet in her hand.

Soviets. Sputnik. Space race.

A meaningless babble of words. If only she could work out how they fitted together.

"Where are they coming from?" Monty repeated, his voice incredulous. "This is Bedlam. The place is filled to the rafters with lunatics. Every dream they dream is a dream of madness."

At Monty's words, a sudden gleam of realization

shone in Penelope's pale green eyes. Maybe the clue was in the dreams themselves. She stared again at the papers in her hand. These were Kemp's dreams. On their own they were incomprehensible, but if they were part of some bigger picture...

She remembered the dimly lit corridor stretching beneath the hospital; the sounds of the sleeping patients rising from their beds to scratch their dreams across countless pages. If she could just see these—find a way to read the puzzling pages in the right order, then she might be able to catch a glimpse of what was causing these unnatural nightmares.

Penelope looked up at Monty, a nervous twitch flitting across the actor's face as he met her determined gaze. "Mr. Maples, must I remind you that the contract you signed committed you to play the part of Montgomery Flinch at his every public appearance."

"Yes, but—"

"And that the fees that we have already paid you cover your services for at least the next week."

"I know, but—"

Penelope raised her hand to cut off the actor's protestations. "There's a story hidden here," she told him, her pale eyes glittering. "An astounding tale of mystery that's ripe for the telling. Montgomery Flinch wouldn't rest until he had found it and neither should we. There's still work to do."

Monty quailed in the face of her certainty.

"But you can't expect me to interview any more of these maniacs," he cried, his hand reaching unconsciously toward his collar. "It's too dangerous. You've seen for yourself how murderously unhinged they are. I'd be lucky to get out of here alive."

Penelope shook her head. "We don't need to speak to them," she replied with a reassuring smile. "We just need to read their dreams."

Monty's brow furrowed and his mouth began to open, but before he could speak, the rotund figure of Dr. Morris barrelled through the door.

"Mr. Flinch! I came as soon as I heard. Thank the Lord that you are unharmed. I had no idea that Kemp was capable of such violence. He's always been a model patient, suffering only from a surfeit of melancholy and these strange delusions of literary fame. It's this terrible affliction that has warped and twisted his emotions." He clasped hold of Monty's hand and fixed him with a gimlet stare. "I only hope you can help us bring an end to this nightmare. Pray tell me, have you made any progress?"

"Well," wheedled Monty, his fingers trying to wriggle out of the doctor's grasp as he groped for an answer, "we think that—that is to say—without making any rash judgements—the difficulty is—"

Penelope cut off Monty's blustering in mid-flow. "Dr. Morris, what my uncle is trying to say is that he first needs to review all of the relevant evidence before he can begin to unravel the mystery behind these sinister events."

"Of course," Dr. Morris exclaimed, gripping Monty's hand more tightly, "just tell me what you need."

"The writings that the patients have made—we'd like to see them," Penelope replied. "All of them."

V

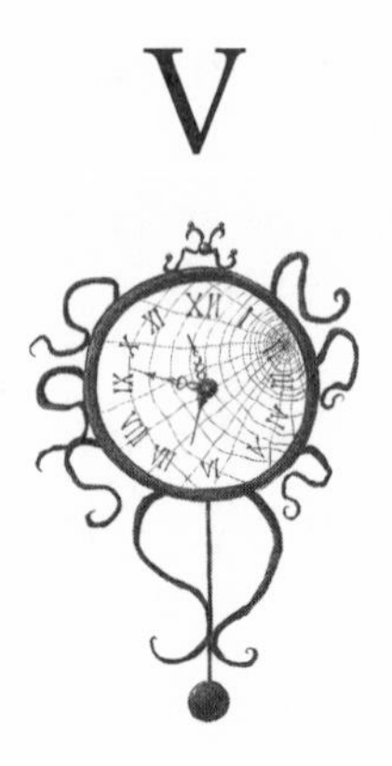

Dr. Morris led Monty and Penelope down a gloomy wood-paneled corridor, their footsteps squeaking across newly polished floorboards as they passed beneath the disapproving stares of the doctor's illustrious predecessors whose dusty portraits hung from the walls.

On her hands and knees in front of them, a young woman in a gray smock-like dress was grimly buffing the floor, the cloth in her hands sticky with wax. She kept her head bowed as the doctor passed, but as Penelope glanced back, the woman raised her eyes to reveal a worn, wrinkled face. A chill shiver crept down Penelope's spine as the woman lifted her hand from her task and pointed toward her with a long, skinny finger, like a witch addressing her victim. Penelope hurriedly turned away, scurrying to catch the doctor's stride as, deep into his monologue, he continued along the corridor.

"As you can see, Mr. Flinch, as part of the

restorative regime in place here at Bethlem Hospital, able-bodied patients are set to work as soon as possible. Making beds, washing laundry, sweeping and polishing the hallways and galleries. We find that through such physical labor, the mind can soonest be mended. However, since the curse that begins at twelve minutes to midnight every night, there are barely enough patients in a fit state for the hospital to function." The doctor traced his finger across a dusty glass case. Beneath the glass stood a forlorn arrangement of wax flowers, their faded petals frozen in an imitation of life. "If things get much worse, soon the only places that we will need to keep swept will be inside the padded cells."

Monty visibly paled as he kept step with the doctor, glancing nervously at the padlocked doors that they passed. "Is it much farther?" he ventured, his hand stealing to his collar again.

"The administrative offices are just this way," Dr. Morris replied, gesturing toward the end of the corridor. "At first we kept the patients' writings with their medical records. A visiting psychiatrist from Vienna, Dr. Freud, claimed that by studying them he could reveal the root causes of the patients' nervous disorders. He said that the strange visions the writings described were symbols that could be decoded to unlock the secrets of the unconscious mind." Dr. Morris let out a snort of derision. "Stuff and nonsense, I thought, but I let him have his head. Dr. Freud spent hours holed up in that office poring over the pages."

"And what did he find?" Penelope asked excitedly as she appeared at the doctor's side.

Dr. Morris glanced down at Penelope, answering her impertinence with a withering stare. "What I said he would find, young lady," the doctor replied, "stuff and nonsense."

He turned back toward Monty to continue his explanation. "Dr. Freud studied the writings of a young newly married woman who had been admitted suffering from bouts of hysteria. She had written of a titanic, unsinkable ship, which was capsized by an iceberg on her maiden voyage, the passengers drowning in the freezing waters of the Atlantic. Dr. Freud claimed that the ship was the young woman's life, the iceberg her new husband, and the drowning passengers her happiness! He said that she wouldn't be cured of her hysteria until she had divorced her husband!" Dr. Morris glowered indignantly over his gold-rimmed glasses. "I sent Dr. Freud packing back to Vienna soon after that."

They were nearing the end of the corridor now, where a dark wooden door stood slightly ajar. Dr. Morris reached out for its handle and pushed the door open to reveal a cramped office filled with desks, pigeonholes, and dusty ledgers.

"Since then the patients' writings have multiplied beyond reason. Every night brings yet more pages filled with their demented babblings. We have had to give over an entire annex of the administrative offices to keep them all. Mr. Jenkins here will be able to show you what you need."

The doctor gestured toward a slight figure in a faded gray suit, who was rising chameleonlike from behind one of the dusty desks. "Jenkins, this is Mr. Montgomery Flinch. Mr. Flinch would like to see the Midnight Papers."

At these last words, Jenkins's mouth twitched, a nervous shadow momentarily flitting across his features as he stepped out from behind his desk.

Dr. Morris turned back toward Monty. "The Midnight Papers is what the orderlies took to calling the patients' nocturnal writings. They joked that they were more believable than the first editions of the *Daily Mail* and the other morning papers."

"Mr. Flinch, it's an honor," said Jenkins, recovering himself as he clasped Monty's hand in his own. "I'm an avid reader of your stories in the *Penny Dreadful.*"

"Why, thank you," Monty nodded his head courteously, "and this is my niece, Miss Penelope Tredwell."

"Miss Tredwell." Jenkins inclined his head toward Penelope in greeting, giving her a first chance to study him at closer quarters. His face was spreading lazily into middle age with jowly cheeks and the beginnings of a double chin as the wattling skin bulged around his neck. His thin lips were pulled uncomfortably into an ingratiating smile, but Penelope noticed that his gray eyes flicked nervously from Dr. Morris to Monty and then back again as if calculating his next move.

"Dr. Morris, if I might just ask," Jenkins ventured, a slight note of shrillness entering his voice. "The Midnight Papers—are you sure? If word was to get out of what is happening to the patients here..."

Dr. Morris fixed him with a glowering stare. "Mr. Jenkins, may I remind you that I am the Physician Superintendent at this hospital. The care and well-being of the patients here is my ultimate responsibility. I believe that Mr. Flinch can help us to bring an end to this nightmare, and I expect you to give him your every assistance. Now bring him the papers."

Jenkins shrank back at the doctor's command. Nodding his head, he turned to rummage in his desk drawer before finally pulling out a large bunch of keys. "We keep the papers in one of the back offices," he told them, motioning for Monty to follow him as he turned toward another door at the rear of the office, half-hidden between the overflowing cubbyholes. "They were taking up far too much space in here—getting mixed up with the patient records and medical notes—so we moved them into the rear annex. We're going to have to find a new space for them soon though." He pushed the door open and ushered them through. "They've practically filled the entire office."

Penelope followed Monty and Dr. Morris as Jenkins led them through a warren of small rooms, each filled with more desks and pigeonholes bristling with papers.

"The patients' writings are kept in here," said Jenkins as he stopped at yet another door and began to search through the loop of keys in his hand. "I'm afraid though that the papers are in some disarray. It's been quite some time since I was able to get to the filing back here." He cast a nervous glance toward Dr. Morris, who scowled back at him owlishly. Finding the right key, Jenkins fitted it to the lock and, turning the handle, began to push the door open. "Here you are, Mr. Flinch—the Midnight Papers."

Penelope heard Jenkins's shocked gasp of surprise but couldn't see its cause as Dr. Morris and Monty stood motionless in front of her, their bulky frames blocking her view of the room's interior.

"Mr. Jenkins," the doctor growled, "what is the meaning of this?"

As Penelope wriggled through the small gap between Monty and the doctor, digging her sharp elbows into Monty's midriff to ease her passage, she heard Jenkins splutter in reply.

"I—I—I don't know."

Through the open doorway, Penelope could see

a small gloomy office, just like all the others they had tramped through. But where the other offices had been crammed to bursting with files and records, papers spilling from every surface, here every pigeonhole was empty, every desk clean; not a single scrap of paper could be seen anywhere.

The Midnight Papers were gone.

VI

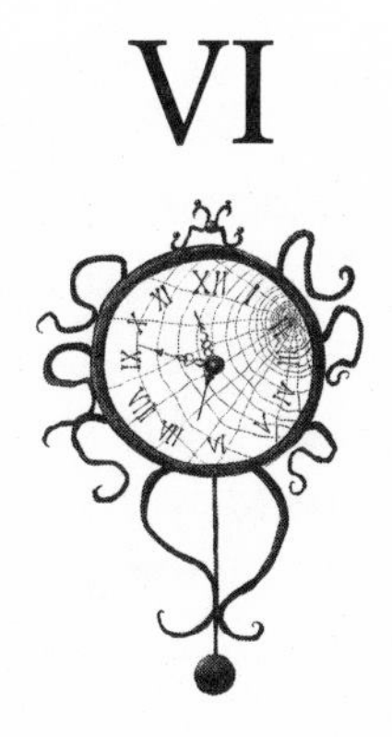

"Where are the patients' writings?" Dr. Morris demanded. "Where are the Midnight Papers?"

Ashen-faced, Jenkins shook his head, his fingers trembling on the door handle as he surveyed the empty office.

"I don't know. They were here first thing this morning—Mr. Bradburn, the night orderly, dropped off the latest batch of writings at the end of his round." He motioned toward the empty desk nearest the door. "I put them there—I was going to try and find the time to file them later today..."

Jenkins's voice trailed away as he shook his head again, dumbstruck by their mysterious disappearance.

"Who else has access to this room?"

At the sound of Penelope's voice, the three men spun in surprise as they turned to face her. She was only a girl, but something in her searching stare compelled Jenkins to answer.

"Just Dr. Morris and myself," he stuttered in reply. "The orderlies bring files and medical notes to the administrative offices, but they never venture past the outer lobby." A momentary flicker of doubt flashed across Jenkins's eyes, but before Penelope could press him further, Monty's booming tones filled the room.

"Well, the mystery deepens, but I'm afraid that without seeing the patients' writings there is little more I can do here now." Monty straightened his jacket and began to turn toward the door that led back to the outer office. "As soon as you gentlemen manage to track down these Midnight Papers, please let me know and I'll return forthwith to solve these strange events. But the next issue of the *Penny Dreadful* will not write itself, so for now I'll bid you good day."

Penelope turned to face Monty, astounded by his audacious attempt to escape from this place. She glared at him in warning, but the actor studiously avoided her gaze. As Dr. Morris fussed around Monty, offering his profuse apologies and assuring him that they would track down the papers, she stood there silently seething. Out of the corner of her eye, she could see Jenkins's pale face flush with relief, but there was nothing she could do about it now.

"Come along, Penelope."

At Monty's imperious command, Penelope gritted her teeth and nodded obediently. Still muttering his apologies, Dr. Morris began to usher them out through the warren of offices.

"I will return shortly, Mr. Jenkins," the doctor called back over his shoulder in a frosty tone, "and we'll discuss this matter further then."

Penelope fumed as she fell into step behind Monty and the doctor, the two men deep in conversation as they left behind the dusty offices to walk back along the long corridors of the asylum. She had been on the brink of a discovery. The nervous flicker in Jenkins's eyes told her that. The patients' writings—these Midnight Papers—they were the key to unlocking this mystery. But Monty's lily-livered constitution hadn't been strong enough to face the challenge of tracking down where they had disappeared to. Now she had to leave behind the scene of potentially her greatest story before the first chapter had even been written.

Ahead of her, the two men stepped to one side in the corridor to let another figure pass. A woman, dressed from head to toe in black, swept by without a word, the veil beneath her widow's cap shrouding the beauty of her features.

"Ma'am," murmured Monty respectfully.

"My lady," intoned Dr. Morris.

Penelope drew to one side too, bowing her head in sympathy as the woman passed. Beneath the flowing lines of her mourning clothes, the woman's youthful figure showed that she had been widowed at a tragically young age. Penelope's eyes followed her along the corridor. What fresh sorrow could bring her to so bleak a place as Bedlam?

As the doctor and Monty resumed their progress along the corridor, Penelope remained where she was standing, her gaze still drawn to the departing figure. With an author's eye, she watched the twilight swish of the widow's weeds; the part of her mind that crafted Montgomery Flinch's fictions seeing the model for a character who could step into the pages of his next story. From behind her, she caught a snatch of Dr. Morris's hushed tones as the two men continued their conversation.

"...quite terrible the tragedy that lady has had to bear—you see, even the finest of families can find themselves touched by the cruel finger of madness..."

The echo of his footsteps obscured the rest of the doctor's words. Penelope watched as the black-veiled lady reached the entrance lobby. Waiting in the shadows there, she glimpsed the burly figure of the scar-faced guard. Her eyes widened in surprise as she watched the widow pause for a moment in front of him. With slender fingers clad in black kid gloves, the widow reached inside her purse and then pressed something into the orderly's hand. Penelope thought she saw an envelope, but in the gloom of the corridor it was difficult to be sure.

As the guard stuffed his hand into his pocket, the veiled woman turned away, gliding like a specter through the entrance doors and out into the world beyond. Intrigued, Penelope stared after her departing figure. A sudden itch in her fingers told her that here was another story, yet more mysteries for her mind to twist into story shape. Penelope's brain whirred with ideas. A widowed wife, a blackmail plot, a dark family secret lost in the corridors of madness. The next issue of the *Penny Dreadful* started to take shape in her mind.

A sudden clattering sound jolted Penelope's thoughts from their plotting. Monty and Dr. Morris were several paces ahead of her, both of them oblivious to the sound as they carried on walking. But as Penelope looked down she saw a metal bucket tipped onto its side, the spilled wax seeping into the floorboards and the wrinkled face of the prematurely aged woman staring up at her.

Penelope quickened her step to pass the woman, but before she could, the woman rose to her feet. Dropping her cloth, she grabbed hold of Penelope's arm with painfully sharp fingers.

"You've got to stop them," she hissed. Her open mouth revealed blackened stumps of teeth. "Stop them before it's too late."

"Please," said Penelope, trying to pull her arm free. "If you could just let me past—"

The woman's nails dug into her skin. "Every night they come, filling my mind with maddening visions. Glimpses of the secrets of the universe revealed."

Penelope stood transfixed, the pain from the nails digging into her skin forgotten as she listened to the woman's pleadings. "But they're watching me, always watching, and when I wake they take my dreams away."

Farther along the corridor, Monty glanced back over his shoulder to check that Penelope was still following. Seeing the patient gripping her arm, he let out a shriek of alarm. At this Dr. Morris turned and, with a shout that rang down the corridor, cried out for assistance.

"Orderly! Orderly!"

Fear flashing across her wrinkled face, the woman pulled Penelope closer. The heavy scent of sweat and waxed floorboards filled the space between them.

"But they can't take them all," she told Penelope, speaking quickly as a thunder of boots echoed down the corridor toward them. She pulled back the sleeve of her gray dress and thrust her bare arm in front of Penelope's face. "See!"

Penelope stared at the liver-spotted skin. The woman's arm was pale and shaking, but scratched in black ink along her veins were the letters $E=MC^2$.

"I don't understand," said Penelope, slowly shaking her head. "What does it mean?"

The woman opened her mouth to reply, but before she could speak, the thunder of footsteps reached a crescendo and the large figure of a white-coated man loomed behind her. With one hand, the man grabbed hold of a handful of hair, and the woman gave an anguished squeal as he dragged her from Penelope's side.

"Leave her alone," Penelope cried.

Still holding the struggling woman by her hair, the burly orderly clamped his other free hand around Penelope's wrist. His fingers tightened and Penelope looked up to see the snarling features of the scar-faced guard.

"It seems you've got the unfortunate knack of upsetting the patients around here," he growled. "I think you'd better leave—for good."

He gave her wrist a vicious twist that made Penelope's eyes sting with tears. As a second orderly reached the hysterical patient and began to bundle her into a stiff side-arm dress, the brutish guard released his grip on Penelope. He turned to help the second guard, the two of them forcing the madwoman into the restraining dress, her arms held captive in its padded pockets.

"Take her to the basement cells, Mr. Bradburn," Dr. Morris ordered, the medic wheezing as he hurried down the corridor toward them with Monty close behind. With a swift nod of his head, the burly guard dragged the woman backward by the collar of her dress, her legs thrashing against the polished floorboards as she let out a banshee wail.

"Are you all right?"

As he reached her side, Monty placed a protective

arm around Penelope's shoulder, blocking her view of the terrible scene.

She slowly nodded her head. The woman's screams echoed down the corridor, but Penelope could still hear the guard's words of warning ringing in her ears. Someone didn't want them here. Closing her eyes, she could see the woman brandishing a shaking arm in front of her face, the strange letters scratched across her skin.

$E=MC^2$

Penelope opened her eyes once again and stared up into Monty's concerned face.

"I'm fine," she replied, "but we're not finished here. We'll be back."

VII

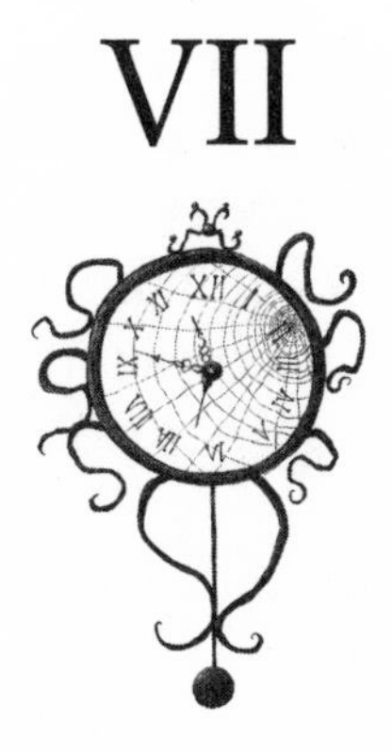

"I'm afraid that Montgomery Flinch isn't here, Mr. Barrett," Penelope replied as she held the door ajar, her face fixed in an apologetic smile. "He is currently secluded in his country manor working on his next fiction serial. I don't think that he will be able to give an interview to your newspaper or indeed any newspaper—exclusive or otherwise."

On the doorstep, the young journalist peered suspiciously past Penelope's shoulder, his gaze trying to penetrate the gloom of the *Penny Dreadful's* office. Inside, two dying gas lamps hung from the ceiling, their fading glow illuminating stacks of magazines and paper proofs piled across desks as the scant December sunlight slowly began to creep in through the office's high windows. At the far desk, the silvery thatch of Penelope's guardian, William Wigram, was bent over a ledger of accounts. The elderly lawyer looked up, raising his eyebrows as Penelope stepped in front of the journalist, blocking his inquisitive stare.

"And I don't suppose you could tell me where Mr. Flinch's country manor can be found?" the journalist asked, scratching doubtfully at his moustache.

Penelope shook her head. "Mr. Flinch is a very private individual," she replied, her cheeks coloring at the thought of revealing such a confidence. "I'm really not at liberty to share his address with passing journalists. He likes to keep the location of his home a secret."

"Seems a lot of things about Montgomery Flinch are secret," the journalist sniffed. "Where he lives, where he was born, where he came from—his readers have a right to know." He peered at Penelope intently. "Anyone would think he had something to hide."

Penelope shifted uncomfortably under the journalist's gaze. "Is that all, Mr. Barrett?"

Blowing out his cheeks, the journalist slowly nodded his head. "For now, but when you next see Montgomery Flinch, please give him this." He handed Penelope his card. "Tell him the *Pall Mall Gazette* would very much like the courtesy of speaking to him to check a few facts, else we might have to run a less than flattering story."

Penelope looked down at the card in her hand.

Mr. Robert Barrett
Arts and Entertainments Correspondent
Pall Mall Gazette
2 Northumberland Street
Strand, London

Pulling the collar of his coat tight against the early morning chill, the journalist turned and headed down the stone steps. As he reached the bottom, he glanced back up at Penelope.

"By the way, it was a clever trick you pulled the other night at the theatre," he said begrudgingly. "Speaking up for Flinch like that—you had everybody fooled. I wonder what they would have said, though, if they knew he was your uncle."

Penelope's smile cracked. The lies she had spun to bring Montgomery Flinch to life now had her trapped in their web.

"That's ridiculous," she spluttered. "Who told you that?"

Barrett tapped the side of his nose conspiratorially.

"A good journalist never reveals his sources," he replied, a wry smile creeping across his face. "But when the bestselling author in Britain pays a visit to Bedlam, well, let's just say people start to talk." He tipped his hat as he turned away. "Good-bye, Miss Tredwell."

Penelope stood frozen for a second, her knuckles whitening around the door handle. Then, with a scowl, she slammed the door shut on Barrett's departing figure.

"Problem?" her guardian asked as Penelope stomped across the office and flung herself into the chair behind her desk.

Penelope shook her head in defiance as she reached for a fresh sheet of foolscap paper.

"Only that journalist from the *Gazette*, he's still digging around for tittle-tattle about Montgomery Flinch. It's nothing that a warning letter to his editor won't solve."

Wigram's forehead creased into its habitual frown, his hooded eyes narrowing as he watched Penelope start to draft her letter.

"I really don't think you should rise to the provocations of the gutter press." He sighed. "I did warn you that giving Montgomery Flinch a more public profile might draw some unwelcome attention."

Penelope looked up from her letter, her fountain pen poised in mid-flow above the paper.

"But we had to do something. Since we published Flinch's first story in the *Penny Dreadful*, the other magazines have been scrambling to keep up with our sales—sending their authors on publicity tours, public readings, even signing sessions. We couldn't risk the public forgetting about Montgomery Flinch."

"I don't think there's any chance of that," her guardian replied with a droll half-smile.

"Have you seen the latest sales figures for the December editions?"

He pushed the ledger he had been studying across to Penelope's desk. Setting her letter to one side, she picked up the ledger, her eyes quickly scanning across the rows of titles and figures.

"*Pearson's* magazine—200,000 copies sold to date, the *Boy's Own Paper*—250,000, the *Strand*—350,000—and that's with the latest Conan Doyle story." Penelope paused, her eyes flashing in a double take across the page. "The *Penny Dreadful*—750,000 copies. That's three quarters of a million!"

"And there's still ten days to go before Christmas," Wigram replied. "When the sales from the provinces are added in, we could be looking at our first million-seller. We've gone to a seventeenth print run already."

A disbelieving grin spread across Penelope's face, her green eyes sparkling with pleasure. The *Penny Dreadful* in a million homes! When she'd first taken over the magazine after her father's death, her only wish had been to keep his memory alive in its pages, a tribute to his unfulfilled dreams of literary stardom. But ever since she'd taken on the pen name of Montgomery Flinch and started filling the pages of the *Penny Dreadful* with her stories, the magazine had become a bestseller. If only her father were still here to see what she'd done.

"Don't you see," she said triumphantly, all thoughts of Barrett's prying flying out of her mind, "that shows that we were right. Montgomery Flinch's first public appearance has pushed sales through the roof. If we can capitalize on this publicity for the next edition of the *Penny Dreadful*, then the sky's the limit."

Her guardian looked at Penelope doubtfully, lines of worry still creasing his forehead.

"Hmm," he mused. "Just remember that all publicity isn't necessarily good publicity."

Behind them, the door handle rattled and Penelope spun around in her chair.

"I've told you, Mr. Barrett, Montgomery Flinch is not here," she yelled. "There will be no interviews today!"

The door slowly opened and two nervously blinking eyes topped by a scruffy mop of blond hair peered around the frame.

"Alfie!"

At Penelope's relieved greeting, the lanky figure of the printer's assistant emerged from behind the door frame. "Morning, Penny, morning, Mr. Wigram."

Closing the door behind him with a click, Alfie stepped toward Penelope's desk, brandishing a copy of the *Times* in his hand.

"I thought you'd want to see this," he told her. "Monty's made it into the papers."

He laid out the newspaper on the desk in front

of Penelope. Quickly turning past the first few pages, he pointed to a headline halfway down one of the dense columns of text on page five.

"Look."

Penelope's heart lurched in her chest as she saw the headline, but as she began to read, her nerves slowly began to settle.

MASTER OF THE MACABRE FINALLY UNMASKED

At the Lyceum Theatre earlier this week, one of the rising stars of London's literary scene finally made his first public appearance. Mr. Montgomery Flinch cut a dashing figure as he took to the stage to give a reading of his very latest tale of terror before its exclusive publication in the December edition of the *Penny Dreadful*. Such was the excitement at this unprecedented event and so numerous was the throng assembled at the doors of the theatre that hundreds were turned away before the reading could commence. Mr. Flinch's astonishing rise to fame and his phenomenal success has convinced many of his literary genius, but until now the man himself has been an enigma. However, his performance on Tuesday evening confirmed his standing as potentially the greatest writer of his age.

Without the aid of artificial amplification, he held the huge auditorium spellbound as he recounted his Christmas chronicle of dread, contriving by the

> modulations of his voice and facial gesticulations to make the characters rise as phantoms before the imagination of his audience. Truly marvelous was the state of suspense created as Mr. Flinch approached the final moments of his story of supernatural betrayal and revenge. So minutely, indeed, were the increasing fear and the gradual advance of death represented by mere force of voice and facial expression that at the close of his tale, several listeners fainted dead away. If this performance is the herald of others to come, Mr. Montgomery Flinch will surely take his place in the coming century as one of the titans of English literature.

"Not bad, eh?" said Alfie, as Penelope looked up in amazement from the newspaper. "And the reviews in the rest of the papers all say the same. Monty's reading has caused quite a stir—people can't wait for the next performance. I reckon you could sell out another ten nights in London alone before the New Year."

Penelope's pale green eyes momentarily glittered at the thought of the sales yet more readings by Montgomery Flinch could bring, but then she winced as she remembered the whereabouts of her leading man. Since the incident at Bedlam, Monty had retreated to his club, drinking away his earnings and keeping a safe distance from Penelope's anger at his cowardly conduct. She shook her head.

"No more performances this year," she said flatly. "We still need to keep a sense of mystery around Montgomery Flinch."

She folded the newspaper in two to hand it back to Alfie, trying to ignore the disappointment on his face, but as she did she noticed another news headline tucked away at the bottom of the page.

BETHLEM HOSPITAL CLOSED TO NEW PATIENTS

Penelope's hand froze in midair as she quickly read the brief report, the text of it only a single sentence long.

> We understand that the Bethlem Royal Hospital has, by order of the Physician Superintendent, Dr. Charles Morris, M.D., F.R.C.P., closed its doors to new admissions until further notice.

She'd tried to put the mysterious events at Bedlam out of her mind, throwing herself into her preparations for writing Montgomery Flinch's next story for the January edition of the *Penny Dreadful*—a suitably sinister tale to greet the new century—but the baffling mystery hidden behind the doors of the asylum still gnawed away at her, and now seeing this headline she was determined to find the answer.

She stood up from her desk.

"I'm going out," Penelope told her guardian as she reached for her cloak hanging from the stand behind her.

Wigram looked up in surprise. "And the new story?" he asked her, his gaze pointedly turning toward the pile of blank pages stacked beside her typewriter.

Drawing her cloak around her shoulders, Penelope swept her long hair back from her face. "I need to do some more research. In fact," she said, turning toward Alfie, who was running his expert eye over the latest set of printer's proofs on her desk, "I could do with some help with this, Alfie—if you could spare a few hours."

Alfie grimaced at the thought of spending his half-day holiday holed up in some dusty library.

"I was thinking of going to see the Hotspurs at White Hart Lane this afternoon," he replied, but looking up from the proofs he saw a devil-may-care smile flash across Penelope's face—a look that held out the promise of adventure. He swiftly nodded his assent. "But I can go along to the football next week. I'll come and help you."

Oblivious to this secret exchange, Wigram shook his head in exasperation as the two of them turned toward the door.

"I'll just hold the fort here then," the elderly lawyer called after them in a withering tone. "The January edition of the *Penny Dreadful* is scheduled to go to press in less than two weeks. There are twenty pages of new fiction to commission, letters to edit, countless illustrations to check. And that's before we even think about the advertising. This periodical won't publish itself, you know."

But his muttered litany of complaints were cut off in mid-flow as Penelope and Alfie closed the front door behind them and hurried down the stone steps to the bustling street below.

"So where are we really going?" Alfie asked, as they pushed their way through the crowds. A hansom cab was clattering over the cobbles toward them and Penelope flung out her hand to hail it. As the cabbie reined his horses to a halt in front of them, she turned to Alfie, her face flushed with excitement.

"Bedlam," she replied with a grin.

VIII

"So you think this Jenkins character has something to do with what's happening to all the patients in there then?"

Penelope shook her head. "I don't know, but he knows something—I'm sure of it. There was fear in his eyes when we arrived in his office and Dr. Morris told him that Monty and I wanted to see the Midnight Papers. He could hardly stop himself from twitching the whole time we were there. And when we discovered the patients' writings had disappeared, I could tell there was something else that he was hiding. I'd have found out what it was, too, if Monty hadn't given up the ghost on the search before we'd had the chance to get it started."

Pinning up her long dark hair, Penelope reached out and took the flat cap from Alfie's hand. She pulled it down over her forehead, the low brim shielding her eyes in disguise. "But we can put that right now."

"And what about this brute of an orderly—Bradburn, was it?" Alfie asked, scratching his uncombed thatch of hair. "Where does he fit into the picture?"

Penelope looked down at her hand at the place where her sleeve ended, the pale, slender strip of skin there marked with a harsh red line where Bradburn had viciously twisted her wrist.

"He didn't want me hanging around to find out."

From a short distance, there came the sound of voices and the two turned to peer through the hospital railings. A straggling line of workers crossed the entrance court, leaving the grand columns of the portico behind them. Penelope saw the burly figure of Bradburn leading the way, his scarred face twisted into a cruel smile as he shared a joke with three more orderlies who flanked his steps. Twenty feet behind them, half-hidden among a stream of other gray-suited office staff, was Jenkins's jowly face, his eyes nervously darting from side to side as they neared the gates.

"It's the end of the morning shift. They're coming out." Hanging back in the shadow of the asylum, Penelope turned back to Alfie. "Remember what we agreed. I'll follow Jenkins and you stick close to Bradburn. Find out where he goes, who he sees. Whatever you do, don't let him catch you following him. He's a nasty piece of work."

"Don't worry about me, Penny," Alfie replied with a grin. "I'll be like the great Sherlock Holmes tracking down the dastardly Professor Moriarty. He'll never see me coming."

Penelope frowned.

"Professor Moriarty murdered Sherlock Holmes at the end of 'The Adventure of the Final Problem'," she reminded him sternly. "Just keep a safe distance and I'll meet you back at the *Penny Dreadful* when we're done."

Glancing up, she saw the departing hospital workers filing out of the gates. Bradburn had stopped for a moment, a copy of The *Sporting Life* newspaper tucked under his arm. As the other three orderlies crowded around him, Penelope strained her ears to catch their conversation.

"Come on, Bradburn," said the youngest of his cronies, a spotty-faced fellow who didn't look much older than Alfie himself, "let us into your secret. How do you keep on picking the right horses? That's seven straight winners you've backed on the trot."

"Wouldn't you like to know," Bradburn sneered. "You'll have to wait until I've got my own stable of horses racing at Ascot—maybe I'll give you a couple of tips then."

"That's a good 'un—you owning a racehorse!" The young orderly's pimply face creased in a grin. "That game's fit for lords and ladies, not the likes of us."

Penelope saw Bradburn's expression change in an instant, his scar whitening as his face flushed red with anger.

"You'll see," he snarled in reply. He shoved his way past the young orderly, who recoiled in fear. "I'm not going to spend the rest of my days clearing out bedpans in Bedlam like you fools will."

Leaving his workmates behind, Bradburn stepped out into the traffic, shouting an angry curse at a dray-cart driver who frantically reined in his horses to avoid a collision. As Bradburn crossed the street in the direction of the Kennington Road, Alfie glanced across at Penelope.

"Wish me luck," he breathed as he set off in close pursuit.

Penelope kept her eyes fixed on the gates of the hospital. From between their white pillars, she saw Jenkins emerge and quickly turn left, scurrying down the Lambeth Road. With the cap pulled low and her cloak wrapped around her, Penelope followed him, keeping to the shadows as she stalked Jenkins's path.

A wintry western wind was blowing in from the river, bringing with it a fog that clung to the sides of the buildings, suddenly shrouding the street in shadows even though it was nearly midday. Passers-by were like gray ghosts shuffling through the smoky, soot-stained air, reaching out to steady themselves as they stumbled half-blinded along the road. Penelope had to quicken her step to keep Jenkins in sight, dodging past the other pedestrians blocking her path as the clerk plunged onward into the gloom.

They were nearing the Thames now, the hum and hiss of life on the river penetrating through the cloaking fog. Penelope heard the clatter of loading barges, their moorings creaking as ropes were pulled tight. Through the smoke and steam, she could just make out the indistinct shapes of steamboats with red and green eyes of fire plying the treacherous pathways of the great river, their shrill horns shaking the air.

Pushing her way through a loitering crowd clustered around a street trader hawking his wares, Penelope fought to keep Jenkins in view. She ignored the thrusting hands of a young beggar clamoring for change as the fog rising from the river thickened around them, blocking her view to only inches ahead.

"Confound it," Penelope fumed, shaking off the urchin as she stumbled onward, her hands scrabbling against the granite wall of the embankment for guidance. Then the wind shifted, and ahead of her in the gloom, she glimpsed Jenkins's portly figure, his dark gray suit almost lost in the fog. He was heading across Lambeth Bridge.

Penelope hurried forward, her footsteps clattering up the steep cobbled approach that led to the bridge. Its ugly iron framework squatted in the mud of the Thames, the wide spans of wire cables curving across the river wreathed in mist. Passing an abandoned tollbooth, Penelope hurried along the footway. Jenkins was some thirty paces ahead of her, his gray figure stepping like a phantom through the smoke and shadows. Penelope quickened her step.

As they neared the far side of the bridge, a line of high chimneys rose out of the fog. Jets of smoke and steam spouted from the dark warehouses and factories, creating a scene that looked more like one of Flinch's visions of Hell than the London Penelope knew. Pulling her cloak across her mouth to shield herself from the stench of industry, she followed Jenkins as he hurried across the cobbles toward the Horseferry Road.

At the corner of the street, an immense shipping advertisement covered the entire side of a building, its once bright colors now streaked with soot and dust. In his gray business suit Jenkins looked oddly out of place as he plunged into the crowd that thronged the square where the river met the road. Rough journeymen loaded carts with sacks and barrels, while dirty-faced boys played leapfrog over broken street posts. In the gutter, a half-naked tramp picked through the rubbish, flinching from the whip crack of a passing carriage. The filthy street was filled with every kind of squalor.

Penelope hurried on, dogging Jenkins's trail as

he fled into the warren of steep streets, heading west. Where was the man going? Ahead of them the traffic had come to a sudden standstill as the load from one cart lay spilled across the cobbles. A gaggle of curious bystanders pressed noisily around the scene, drawn by the clash of wheels and hooves. As the two drivers exchanged threats, the clamor from the crowd rose at the promise of violence.

The pavement narrowed as Penelope tried to elbow her way through the press. Stepping into the road, she winced as her boot slipped in the steaming ordure left by the horses. Her anger rising, she pushed her way through the crowd, just in time to see Jenkins disappearing through the doors of a dingy public house.

Penelope looked up at the shabby sign hanging above its entrance—the Three Crowns—but from the dirt-encrusted windows and the two drunks slumped in the gutter outside, she could tell that this wasn't an establishment favored by the aristocracy.

She had to find out what business Jenkins had there. Pulling the cap farther down over her face, she stepped toward the door of the tavern. Then she felt a hand grab at her shoulder and a voice whisper in her ear.

"Penny!"

She wheeled in surprise to see Alfie emerging from the shadows.

"What are you doing here?" she hissed. "I told you to follow Bradburn!"

"I did," Alfie replied. "He's inside the pub. I was going to follow him, but then I saw Jenkins arriving too."

He cast a nervous glance over his shoulder at one of the drunks, who had now staggered noisily to his feet. The stumpy man lurched toward them with an outstretched hand, the sleeve of his threadbare brown overcoat flailing as he begged for change.

"Spare us a couple of pennies for a pint," he slurred.

Penelope ignored the man, her gaze firmly fixed on the door to the pub. "We've got to go inside—find out what they're doing there."

Alfie shook his head as he looked down at Penelope's clothes: the fine embroidery embellishing her black cloak with its fur-lined collar and velvet trim. Even though her boots were muddied and worse, they were still recognizably fashionable.

"You can't go in there looking like that," he told her. "They'll spot you straightaway."

"Drink!" the drunken man demanded as he tugged on Alfie's arm.

Penelope scowled, anxious not to waste anymore time on the tavern's doorstep while the answer to Bedlam's mystery could be uncovered inside.

"So what are we supposed to do?"

IX

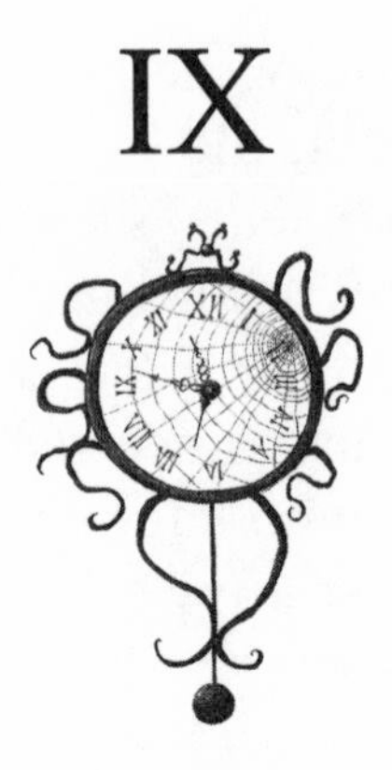

The pub was crowded. Dingy red curtains were half-drawn across its small cobwebbed windows, peering like two bloodshot eyes at the darkness within. A motley mob of rivermen, vagrants, and thieves thronged the long room, the taller among them stooping their heads beneath the low ceiling. A scrum of figures hemmed in the bar at the far end, squeezing their elbows between the empty gin measures, ale quarts, and glasses piled up on the metal counter as they shouted their orders at the barmaid. In reply, her mouth snapped open with a snaggletoothed leer as she slopped another round of drinks in front of them.

The brim of the cap pulled low over her eyes, Penelope looked down at the long brown overcoat she was wearing, her own clothes hidden beneath. It smelled as if something had died inside, but the itch crawling down her back made her fear that something was still alive. Alfie led the way as they pushed through the press of people.

"Where are they?" she hissed in Alfie's ear, as she stepped over the lolling figure of a pale thin man, his threadbare pockets turned out and emptied.

Before Alfie could answer, Penelope felt a hand snake into her own pocket, its fingers grasping in search of a purse. Swiftly turning, she grabbed hold of the hand before it had the chance to slip away. Struggling to free himself, a scrawny boy stared up at Penelope, his eyes filled with defiance.

"Keep your hair on," he whined, "I didn't take nothing."

The boy was only a year or so younger than Penelope, the top of his head reaching up to her shoulder. He was dressed in an ill-fitting jacket that hung down to his knees, its bulging pockets hinting at the things he had already pilfered.

"You were trying to rob me," Penelope replied indignantly.

At the sound of her cut-glass accent, the boy started in surprise. He caught a glimpse of the fine embroidery hiding beneath the collar of Penelope's overcoat.

"You're a proper bit of frock, aren't you," he hissed. "Well, don't think you can rub me into the peelers."

Before Penelope had a chance to respond, the boy kicked out, his boot striking her ankle. With a yelp of pain, Penelope released her grip on his hand and the boy darted back into the crowd, disappearing among the throng of drinkers.

"Are you all right?" asked Alfie, glancing back in concern. Around them, the shrieks and bellows of the crowd had swallowed Penelope's cry of pain, nobody paying it the slightest bit of attention.

Penelope nodded, a blush of embarrassment rising to her cheeks.

"I'm fine," she replied through gritted teeth, ignoring the throb of her ankle. "Let's find Bradburn and Jenkins."

With a grin, Alfie motioned toward a hodgepodge of beer-stained tables clustered around a miserable-looking fire. At one, Jenkins sat glumly sipping a mug of ale, while the burly frame of Bradburn loomed over him. From beneath the brow of her cap, Penelope could see the orderly's lips moving in a constant snarl, but she couldn't hear a single word over the babble of voices that filled the room.

"We've got to get closer," she said.

Keeping her head low, Penelope bustled her way toward the fireplace and then hunkered down at a table a few feet away, her back to the two men. As Alfie joined her, she strained her ears to make out the sound of their voices.

"But where are the papers?" Jenkins whined. "We agreed—I'd let you take a handful at a time as long as you returned most of them the very next day, but the entire office was empty."

The low growl of Bradburn's voice cut the clerk's whine into silence.

"They're safe, that's all you need to know. And you keep your mouth shut, unless you want Dr. Morris to find out how all those patients' valuables ended up in a Drury Lane pawnbroker's shop."

Penelope heard Jenkins splutter in protest.

"Now where are last night's papers?" Bradburn demanded.

There was a rustling sound. Penelope risked a swift glance over her shoulder to see Jenkins pull out a thin brown envelope from inside his jacket and hand it over to Bradburn's grasping hand.

"Where are the rest of them?" the orderly snarled.

"This is all I could get," Jenkins moaned in reply. "Since the Midnight Papers disappeared, Dr. Morris has set up a new system for collecting the patients' writings. He's now keeping them in the safe in his own office. These are all I could take before he locked them away."

Bradburn let out an angry growl.

"Well, you need to try harder next time," he warned him. There came a harsh squealing sound as the orderly pushed back his chair from the table and rose to his feet. "Remember: if you break our agreement, then I'll break your neck."

In the grimy reflection from a discarded tankard, Penelope watched as Bradburn shoved his way through the heaving throng before his burly frame disappeared out the door to the street beyond. Left alone at the table, Jenkins buried his head in his hands with a choking sob.

"You stay here with him," Penelope whispered to Alfie. "I want to see where Bradburn goes now."

Leaving Alfie to keep watch over the clerk's dejected figure, she quickly left the pub. Bradburn was already some thirty paces ahead, striding purposefully up the road. Slipping the threadbare overcoat from her shoulders, Penelope dropped it back beside its owner, who was still slumped in the gutter but now happily clutching a bottle of gin.

The fog was starting to lift, but Penelope stuck close to the shadows as she followed Bradburn's trail. He was leaving the streets of the riverside slums behind as he headed west in the direction of the more genteel districts of Knightsbridge and South Kensington. The crisp, clean crowds of businessmen and ladies of leisure parted with disdain as Bradburn's coarse figure passed, but the orderly didn't even glance back as he strode grimly on.

Keeping him in sight, Penelope hurried down the wide promenade, the shops and houses becoming grander with every step she took. A young gentleman tipped his hat to her as she passed and Penelope felt herself beginning to relax. In the distance, the grand buildings of the Victoria and Albert Museum rose high above the Cromwell

Road, the sweeping curves of its architecture partly obscured by scaffolding. Beyond this, lay the British Museum of Natural History, the Imperial Institute, and the Royal Albert Hall. She shook her head. This was her territory. What was Bradburn doing here?

On the opposite side of the road stood a grand redbrick house, its tall windows and fanlights looking down condescendingly at the passing traffic. Bradburn hurried across the road, darting behind a speeding omnibus. Opening the gate, he scurried up the stone steps that led to the front door. Crossing the road after him, Penelope sheltered behind the manicured hedge that fronted the property, peeking between its leaves to see what would happen next. She was surprised to see Bradburn ignore the tradesmen's bell and instead loudly rap twice on the door knocker, the sound of it echoing behind the dark green door.

After a pause, the front door slowly opened and a butler peered out inquisitively. Bradburn spoke briefly, but from behind the hedge Penelope couldn't make out the words. Then her suspicion grew as she watched the butler quickly usher him inside. The door closed with a slam.

Penelope took a step backward, looking up at the grand façade of the house. Her eyes swept past its windows and wrought-iron balconies, reaching up for five stories into the darkening sky. *It must be worth over ten thousand pounds,* Penelope thought. *What on earth was a two-bob orderly doing here?*

"Pardon me, Miss."

A delivery boy was wheeling a heavily laden barrow along the narrow pavement.

"Excuse me," said Penelope as she stepped to one side to let him pass. "Do you know whose house this is?"

The young boy glanced up at the redbrick building and sniffed.

"'Course I do," he replied. "That's where the Spider Lady of South Kensington lives."

X

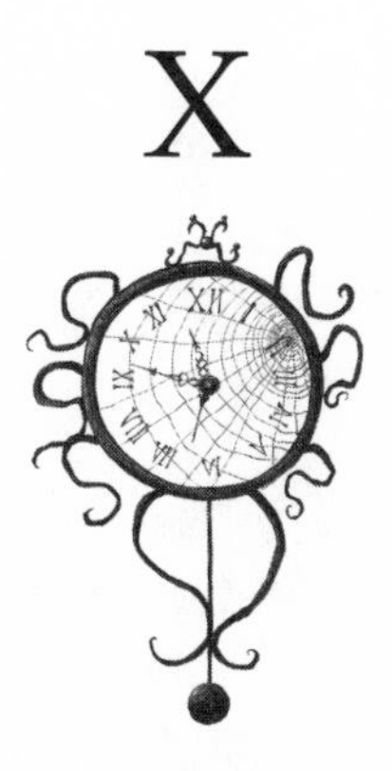

Penelope leafed through the pages of *Who's Who*, her eyes scurrying over the entries as she searched out the one she was looking for. Next to her on the reading desk sat a stack of reference books: *Burke's Peerage, Kelly's Handbook to the Titled Classes,* and other assorted guides to the aristocracy. She leaned forward on the hard mahogany chair, the electric reading light above the desk spilling a warm yellow glow across the pages. From around her came the sound of scratching pens and turning pages, the long rows of desks fanning out around the room filled with readers. Countless rows of books ran along the walls and gave the library the snug feel of her home.

Penelope's fingers paused as they turned the next page, her eye snagging on the entry in the top right-hand corner.

CAMBRIDGE, Lady; Isabella Violet Hester

Born 13 Nov. 1876; daughter of Sir William Ross,

FRCS (died 1897) and Lady Marie Charlotte Ross; married in 1897 to Lord Cambridge (died 1898)

Education

Cheltenham Ladies' College; King's College, University of London

Career

Travelled extensively in Europe, India, and Africa, conducting entomological research into exotic species of arachnids; appointed to the board of trustees of the British Museum of Natural History

Publications

Untangling the Web: Observations about Arachnid Behavior, 1897; *Taxonomic Notes of the Spider Fauna of Southern India*, 1895; *A Morphological Study of Spider Toxins and Venom*, 1898; scientific papers and journals, chiefly on arachnology

Recreation

Reading, cross-stitch, and embroidery

Address

Stanley House, 2 Egerton Gardens, South Kensington, London

So this was who Bradburn had been calling on, mused Penelope as she glanced up from the book, a puzzled expression written across her face. Lady Isabella Cambridge—the Spider Lady of South Kensington. But what interest could this aristocratic lady have in a hard-faced orderly from Bedlam, his pocket filled with the patients' scribblings? She sighed in frustration, causing the reader at the next desk, an old bespectacled man, to shush her in irritation.

Penelope frowned. She looked back down at the entry from *Who's Who*, her eyes settling on the details of Lady Cambridge's career. A life described in a couple of lines, but she needed to find out more. She painstakingly reread the entry, searching for some clue that could help her—

> traveled extensively...research into exotic species of arachnids...appointed to the board of trustees of the British Museum of Natural History...author of numerous scientific papers.

Penelope clicked her fingers in a sudden rush of realization.

"Hush!"

Ignoring the bookish chorus of shushes, Penelope grinned in satisfaction. There was one place she could go to find out more about the mysterious Lady Cambridge. It was time to pay a visit to the museum.

"This most remarkable specimen is a new genus of the *Mantichora*, the African tiger beetle. You will see, of course, the mottled green markings on the surface of its shell, a sharp contrast to the uniformly black coloring usually found in beetles of this genus. Note, too, the large curved mandibles which the African tiger beetle uses to seize and crush its prey."

The gray-bearded professor pointed with his brass-tipped cane to the image of the emerald beetle which shone from the screen behind him. As he prodded at its sickle-shaped jaws, Penelope half hoped that the magnified image of the beetle would spark into life and snap the cane in two. Sitting on the desk at the front of the great hall, the episcope projector whirred noisily, its mechanical drone almost drowning out the professor's dry as dust voice. Next to this, yet more insect specimens were lined up, ready for their turn in the spotlight.

Penelope stifled a yawn. She glanced down again at the notice she had torn from the newspaper.

> A Public Lecture on the Entomological Discoveries of the 1899 British Empire Africa Expedition will be given by Professor Alfred Stebbing in the Central Hall of the British Museum of Natural History, on Monday, 18 December, at 8.30 p.m. The Right Hon. Sir Edwin Lancaster will chair the lecture and the museum's board of trustees will be in attendance.

Peering back over her shoulder, Penelope scanned the great hall yet again, searching for any sign of the enigmatic Lady Cambridge. Countless rows of chairs stretched back across the mosaic floor, their seats filled with bearded faces. Young men with dark, wiry whiskers, elderly gentlemen with white, fluffy beards; not a single face belonged to a member of the fairer sex. Above their heads, the hall's high-vaulted ceiling was lit with an amber glow, sculptures of terra-cotta monkeys scampering across its soaring arches. At the front of the hall, behind the lecturer's raised stage, a central stone staircase swept up to the galleries above.

As yet another hideously enlarged insect filled the screen, Alfie sneaked back into the empty chair next to Penelope at the end of the front row. He had dressed for the occasion, with a borrowed suit jacket and tie covering most of the ink stains on his shirtfront. Tugging uncomfortably at this tie as he settled in his seat, Alfie turned toward Penelope.

"Have you found her?" she asked him, her voice low to avoid the hushes of the audience around them.

Alfie shook his head. "I've been up and down every row. The place is packed to the rafters, but the only woman I saw was a charlady dusting the exhibits at the back of the hall." A cheeky grin crept across his face. "I don't think that could have been your Lady Cambridge."

"But she's on the museum's board of trustees." Penelope frowned. "The advertisement said they'd be here."

"Maybe she got bored and went home." Alfie nodded toward the professor as he fussed over the episcope. "I mean that feller don't half go on a bit."

On the screen behind the projector, the image of a large black spider with strange silver markings across its back slowly flickered and faded to black. For a moment there was silence as the whir of the episcope died away, then Professor Stebbing stepped back from the machine and the audience in the hall broke into a polite round of applause.

Leading the plaudits, a portly gentleman in a long frock coat rose from the front row and stepped onto the lecture stage. His jowly face was clean-shaven except for a pair of gray-whiskered sideburns that crept across his cheeks like inquisitive caterpillars. Penelope recognized him straightaway from his portrait hanging in the Central Hall—Sir Edwin Lancaster, the director of the museum.

As he motioned for quiet, Sir Edwin's voice boomed out across the great hall.

"I would like to thank Professor Stebbing for the learned insights he has shared with us this evening. Many more samples from the British Empire Africa Expedition are still to be unboxed and cataloged and once this task has been completed, then perhaps we will have the pleasure of hearing more about the fascinating creatures that creep across that vast continent."

Lifting his head, he gestured up toward the pillars of the first-floor gallery that looked down on the great hall. The eyes of the audience followed his gesture and Penelope saw with surprise a row of figures seated behind the balustrade.

"I would also like to extend my thanks to the board of trustees for their support of this expedition," Sir Edwin continued. "Its success was due in no small part to their contributions, in particular the very generous donation that Lady Cambridge made to the expedition funds."

Penelope strained her eyes against the lights that hung beneath the gallery. She could just make out the figure of a lone woman seated among the beards and stuffed shirts of the other trustees. The woman was dressed in a stiff-necked black gown, her face half hidden by shadows, but Penelope still caught a glimpse of her youthful beauty. It was the same face she had last glimpsed beneath a veil in the corridors of Bedlam.

"Now as this evening draws to a close," declared Sir Edwin, clasping his hands together as he looked out over the audience, "all that there remains for me to say is to wish each of you a very merry Christmas and a happy new year. Good night and God bless."

Another round of applause rippled through the great hall, as the audience slowly rose to their feet. They began to shuffle toward the stone archway at the rear of the hall, eager to be the first in line for the hansom cabs waiting at the exit. Penelope kept her eyes fixed on the figure of Lady Cambridge.

While the other trustees stayed in their seats, Lady Cambridge had risen to her feet. With a cursory nod, she bade them farewell, then turned and walked along the gallery.

As Lady Cambridge's shadowy figure flitted between the gothic pillars, Penelope rose to her feet. "Come on, we've got to follow her."

While the straggling crowd headed for the exit, Penelope led Alfie in the opposite direction. They skirted the stage at the front of the hall where Sir Edwin was deep in conversation with Professor Stebbing, neither of the two men noticing them as they slipped past. As they reached the bottom of the grand stone staircase, Penelope squinted up into the shadows that lined the long gallery, desperately trying to keep Lady Cambridge in sight.

She caught a glimpse of a black gown behind a glass case filled with stuffed birds. The long gallery was lined with exhibits—ancient fossils and pickled crocodiles, human skulls and dinosaur bones—and Lady Cambridge flitted through the shadows like some silent predator.

But as Penelope stepped onto the stone staircase in pursuit, the sound of a man's voice stopped her dead in her tracks.

"Miss Tredwell!"

Penelope turned around to see the lean figure of the *Pall Mall Gazette's* Arts and Entertainments Correspondent, Mr. Robert Barrett. An intrigued half-smile played across the reporter's lips as he stepped toward them, his fountain pen hovering above the open notebook in his hand.

"What an unexpected surprise to see you here this evening."

XI

"I wouldn't have thought that a young lady of your refinement would be interested in a lecture about creepy-crawlies from the wilds of Africa." As he spoke, Barrett's eyes flicked past Penelope and Alfie, his gaze wandering up the staircase as if in search of someone else. "Has your uncle brought you here tonight? I must admit, I hadn't spotted the famous Montgomery Flinch in the audience. Was he keeping watch from the gallery while he researched his next tale of terror?"

Penelope returned the young journalist's smile, trying to hide her irritation at this unexpected obstacle in their path.

"Good evening, Mr. Barrett," she replied. "No, I'm afraid my uncle isn't here this evening. He's still ensconced at his house in the country working on a new story. The British Empire Africa Expedition is of no interest to him."

"That's a pity," Barrett sniffed. "I thought I might

have an exclusive about how Montgomery Flinch's next fiction serial will be an African adventure to rival the stories of H. Rider Haggard."

Penelope shook her head. "You'll have to wait until the new century and the next edition of the *Penny Dreadful* to find that out." She glanced up at the gallery above, catching a glimpse of Lady Cambridge's silhouetted figure as she swept past the top of the staircase. "Now if you'll excuse me, there's someone that I have to speak to."

Barrett followed Penelope's gaze as Lady Cambridge disappeared behind the first of the pillars that lined the facing gallery.

"Ah, the reclusive Lady Cambridge," he sighed. "The only person in London society who makes your uncle look like an extrovert. Good luck in getting to speak to her."

As Alfie shuffled his feet impatiently, Penelope glanced back at Barrett in surprise.

"You know Lady Cambridge?" she asked.

Barrett grinned. "Not personally," he replied. "But as a journalist on the *Gazette*, I've chronicled her many triumphs. The first woman to jointly lead a scientific expedition into the heart of Africa, the discoverer of dozens of new species of insects and spiders that have transformed man's understanding of the natural world, and now, of course, she's the first female trustee in the history of the museum. Her father would be so proud."

"Her father?"

"Sir William Ross. He was the director of this museum for more than two decades. It's such a shame that he never got to see any of his daughter's achievements. Sir William died on the eve of her wedding to Lord Cambridge."

Penelope felt a fleeting pang of sympathy; the death of Lady Cambridge's father suddenly reminding her of her own loss.

"Some say it was the shock of his passing that sent Lady Cambridge's mother into the arms of madness," Barrett continued. "But of course, Lady Cambridge has had her own tragedy to bear since then. The death of her husband, Lord Cambridge, on expedition in Africa—poisoned by the very spiders they had both gone there to study. On her return to England, Lady Cambridge retreated into her widow's weeds and she hasn't been seen in public for more than a year. Until tonight..."

Barrett left this revelation hanging in the silence of the great hall. He glanced back toward the stage where Professor Stebbing was showing the portly Sir Edwin one of his many specimens, the two men deep in conversation as the professor held the insect to the light.

"And my report of tonight's lecture won't be complete without a quote from Professor Stebbing and maybe even Sir Edwin Lancaster himself. I'll bid you both good night now." With a nod of farewell, Barrett turned as if to leave. He took a couple of steps toward the stage, but then glanced back as if suddenly remembering something.

"Please don't forget to ask your uncle to contact me at the *Gazette* on his return to the city," he told Penelope. "The story I'm writing about Montgomery Flinch's remarkable rise to fame is throwing up a few mysteries of its own. An exclusive interview with the man himself might help to clear these up for our readers."

With that, Barrett turned away again, hurrying toward the stage where the professor and museum director were still deep in conversation.

For a moment, Penelope stood there silently fuming. The last thing she needed was some meddling journalist poking around in the dark corners of Montgomery Flinch's invented life. *How would the readers of the* Penny Dreadful *react if they discovered that Flinch didn't really exist?* Penelope frowned. There had to be a way out of this predicament, but first she had her own mystery to solve.

"Come on," she said, tugging at Alfie's arm. "We can still find her."

Penelope raced up the staircase with Alfie close behind, their footsteps clattering up the stone steps. Under the disapproving gaze of Charles Darwin's statue, the two turned right to climb the final flight of stairs. There, blocking their path, stood a thin, sharp-featured man. He was wearing the drab uniform of a museum attendant and his beady stare flicked from Penelope to Alfie in turn.

"The museum is closed," he said coldly. "Please make your way back to the exit."

Her heart sinking, Penelope glanced past him into the shadows of the gallery above. Lady Cambridge might only be yards away—she couldn't let this jumped-up bone-watcher stand in her way. As the guard fixed them with a frosty stare, Penelope racked her brain for a way to get past him. The only thing she could think to try was a barefaced lie.

She turned toward Alfie, tipping him a sly wink before she let rip with an almighty howl.

"But Daddy said we could see the dinosaurs!"

The museum guard's stony features cracked in the face of her brattish whine. With a long-suffering sigh, he tried to quieten her.

"Now, young lady, there's really no need for such a hullaballoo. The museum opens again at ten tomorrow and I'm sure you'll be able to see the dinosaurs then."

Penelope glared up at him, her reddening face screwed up like a spoiled child's. "If you don't let me see the dinosaurs right away, then I'm going to tell my daddy how perfectly beastly you are."

The attendant stared back at her in disbelief. "And who exactly might your father be?" he sniffed dismissively.

With a haughty toss of her hair, Penelope

glanced back down to the lecture stage below. There, the director of the museum was still quizzing Professor Stebbing, while Barrett waited at a respectful distance for his chance to speak to them. She turned back to fix the museum guard with her sternest stare.

"Sir Edwin Lancaster," she answered coolly.

The museum guard blanched at her reply, the color draining from his face. His gaze switched from Penelope to Sir Edwin and then back again. His brow furrowed, and then, with an apologetic expression etched on his face, he stepped to one side and waved Penelope and Alfie through.

"I'm terribly sorry for the misunderstanding, Miss Lancaster," he groveled. "You'll find the iguanodon bones halfway down the gallery in the second bay on the right. Please take as long as you need."

With a harrumph of displeasure, Penelope hurried past the attendant with Alfie following close behind, fighting to keep a smile from his face. Racing up the final flight of stairs, they reached the long gallery which ran along the length of the great hall.

Staring into the shadows, Penelope headed for the place where she had last seen Lady Cambridge. Beneath terra-cotta arches intertwined with climbing snakes, the two walked in silence, their footsteps echoing in the empty exhibition space. The skeleton of a saber-toothed tiger lurked menacingly in the shade, its claws extended as if to swipe at them as they passed. Penelope peered past the glass-fronted cases, each of them filled with innumerable insects, spiders, crustaceans, and centipedes. A stuffed polar bear loomed in the gloom, but no living soul could be seen. Lady Cambridge was gone.

As Penelope and Alfie passed by the fossilized bones of the iguanodon, they heard the pointed sound of a cough behind them. Turning, they saw the museum attendant standing at the top of the gallery landing. Next to him, his arms folded sternly across his barrel chest, stood Sir Edwin Lancaster. The look of fury on both their faces told Penelope that visiting time was over.

"We're going to have to leave," said Alfie, raising his hand in apology.

Penelope sighed. She had come here to find out more about Lady Cambridge, but the woman herself seemed to have vanished into thin air. The mysteries were piling up and she was no closer to finding any answers.

As Penelope turned to leave, her gaze fell on a large display case. Underneath the glass, several rows of spiders were pinned and mounted, each hairy-legged beast staring out at her with an octad of black, beady eyes: a mocking reminder of the elusive Spider Lady of South Kensington.

"Penny," Alfie tugged at her arm, "we have to go now."

Lost in thought, Penelope tried to trace the tangled web that had led her to Lady Cambridge: the strange malady afflicting every patient in Bedlam, the missing Midnight Papers, Bradburn's mysterious visit to her grand house in South Kensington. She remembered seeing the black-veiled widow glide through the corridors of the asylum and something that Barrett had said snagged in her mind.

Her father...Sir William Ross...Some say it was the shock of his passing that sent Lady Cambridge's mother into the arms of madness.

As Alfie tugged on her arm again, a sudden gleam appeared in Penelope's eye—the same gleam that shone whenever she came up with an audacious plot twist. There was one person who could tell her more about Lady Cambridge, someone who knew her better than anyone else—her own mother. And Penelope now knew where she would find her.

XII

His pimply brow knitted in a frown, the young orderly stared at Penelope. The key in his hand hovered in front of the keyhole, but for the moment, the door to the cell remained locked. With his free hand, the orderly nervously scratched at his cheek.

"I don't know if I can let you see her, miss," he said finally. "Dr. Morris's instructions were quite clear. He said that I was to let you and your uncle visit any patient you liked, but now you tell me that Mr. Flinch isn't even coming. It's not right for you to be here alone—you're just a girl."

The prim smile Penelope had kept fixed to her face from the moment she had arrived at Bedlam again tightened in reply. The telegram she had sent in the name of Montgomery Flinch from the offices of the *Penny Dreadful* had got her this far, but with Monty still holed up in his club, and this orderly, who was only a handful of years older than she was, standing in her way, it looked as if she might not get any farther. There was only one card she had left to play.

"I'm so grateful for your concern," Penelope simpered, clasping her hands to her purse. "But my uncle was quite adamant that his absence today shouldn't delay the work that Dr. Morris has tasked him to do. I'm fully aware of the questions he wanted to ask this patient and will report back to him straightaway. My uncle said that if there was any kind of problem, I should give you this envelope."

Penelope drew out a plain white envelope from the depths of her purse and handed this to the orderly. As he opened it, she kept her face composed into an expression of the upmost innocence as she watched the orderly's eyes widen in surprise.

Beneath the flap of the envelope, was a five-pound note—nearly half a year's wages to him. As a blush rose in his cheeks, the orderly quickly closed up the envelope and stuffed it into the pocket of his trousers.

Avoiding Penelope's eye, he fumbled for his keys again, fitting one to the lock and then placing his hand on the handle.

"Ten minutes, that's all you can have," he muttered. "And you need to be careful of this one. Most of the time she's meek as kittens, but if she's upset, you'll hear her snarl."

He turned the handle and the door to the cell slowly swung open.

"I'll be waiting right outside. If she starts to give you any trouble, you just call."

Penelope nodded in reply. Her heartbeat quickened as she stepped into the cell.

From a high barred window, faint rays of sunlight fell into the dismal room, its dusty furnishings laid out like a servant's bedroom. A wooden bedstead covered in a faded counterpane, a chest of drawers, a washstand, and a dressing table. Next to this table, turned half away from her, was an armchair, and in this sat a black-veiled figure. A shiver ran down Penelope's spine as the door closed behind her.

For a moment, Penelope thought that it was Lady Isabella Cambridge herself. Then, with a rustle of black crêpe, the veil was pulled back and, as the figure turned toward her, Penelope found herself staring into the face of an old woman. Her wrinkled skin was as pale as parchment and the woman's blue eyes gleamed like faded sapphires as they slowly focused on Penelope.

From the snatched glance at Lady Cambridge Penelope had caught at the museum, the family resemblance was unmistakable. This was her mother—the Right Honorable Lady Marie Charlotte Ross.

She was wearing a lusterless dress, the black linen faded to charcoal in places, and its crêpe cuffs and collars crumpled with age. The grief that had brought her here to Bedlam showed in every stitch that she wore. As Lady Ross leaned forward in her chair to peer at Penelope, a single strand of white hair escaped from beneath her widow's cap.

"Who is it?" she asked in a quavering voice. "Is that you, Izzy?"

Her heart still thumping in her chest, Penelope stepped out of the shadows.

"No, my lady," she replied. "My name is Penelope Tredwell."

She walked toward Lady Ross, her eyes taking in the widow's possessions hoarded on the dressing table beside her: a lacquered hairbrush, a looking glass, and a framed photograph which showed a distinguished-looking gentleman and a young girl. Behind his whiskers, the man's face was set in a stern frown as he stared into the camera lens, while the girl gazed up adoringly at him.

"You must be one of Izzy's friends then," said Lady Ross, shaking her head in confusion. "Well, I can't have you girls under my feet now—your father will be home from the museum soon."

Penelope stared at the frail lady in sympathy as the realization dawned. In the disorder of her mind, Lady Ross thought that her daughter was still a young girl and her husband still alive. She lifted her palsied fingers from the chair, her hand shaking as she shooed Penelope away.

"Run along now."

Penelope stood her ground, her thoughts racing as she tried to decide what to do. She'd spent most of the *Penny Dreadful's* petty cash to get in here today; she had to try to make her visit worthwhile. Maybe somewhere in Lady Ross's mind there was a fragment of information that could help her, something that might explain what Lady Cambridge's connection to these strange events actually was.

"Your daughter is the reason I'm here," Penelope began. "I want to talk to you about Lady Cambridge."

At the mention of this name, the old woman sank back in her chair, her eyes suddenly filling with tears. "Don't hurt me, Isabella," she whimpered. "I did what you asked. Don't make me take the medicine again."

Aghast, Penelope watched as the old woman shook in her chair, her withered hands gripping the armrests as the floodgates of her madness opened in a babbling flow.

"Just take me away from this place," Lady Ross moaned. "Every night they torture me in my sleep. I've seen you, Izzy, my own flesh and blood in the cell next to mine."

In the midst of her raving, the woman's quavering voice changed, a harsh new tone entering her words as if somebody else was speaking them.

"I'll never be like you, Mother," she snarled. Lady Ross turned toward the dressing-room table and pointed an accusing finger at her own reflection in the looking glass. "We may both have lost our husbands, but only you have lost your mind."

She raised her hand in anger, and then reeled as if struck by the same blow.

"Lady Ross," Penelope cried, reaching out a hand to calm her agitation.

"Don't touch me," the old woman shrieked. She grabbed hold of Penelope's wrist, her bony grip unnaturally strong. "You're trying to poison me—just like all the rest."

As Penelope struggled to free herself, the old woman spat in her face.

"I can hear them," she hissed as the door to the cell slammed open, the orderly racing to Penelope's aid, "the spiders crawling inside my mind."

The orderly wrenched the old woman's fingers from Penelope's wrist, and threw Lady Ross back into the depths of her chair from where she let fly a volley of curses. Reaching into his pocket, he pulled out a small brown bottle and, uncorking this, pressed it to the old woman's lips. Lady Ross struggled, but the orderly held the bottle firmly in place until it was drained; only a fraction of the brownish liquid dribbling from her lips and staining her chin.

As he straightened, the orderly glanced back at Penelope, who had retreated, horrified, to the door.

"You need to go now, miss," he said as Lady Ross slumped in her chair, her eyes rolling back in her head. "Visiting time is over now."

A low moan escaped from Lady Ross's lips, her ravings now reduced to an insensible mumble.

"The spiders...the spiders..."

Penelope turned and fled. She pulled out her handkerchief as she hurried away down the corridor, her only thought to escape from this loathsome place. But as she wiped the spittle from her cheek, Penelope couldn't escape the image of Lady Ross's snarling face that was burned into her mind.

The woman was truly deranged—that much was clear. No hope of finding any clues from her about how Lady Cambridge was tied up with this mystery—only ravings about spiders and poison. The madness that stalked these walls had already overwhelmed her. Penelope's visit here had been in vain.

As she reached the entrance lobby, she glanced across at the spot where she had seen Lady Cambridge pause in front of the scar-faced guard. She remembered the envelope that had passed between them. What secrets had it held? The mystery of Bedlam still remained and if she couldn't solve it, then Montgomery Flinch's latest tale would remain unwritten.

She only had one option left—to pay a visit to Lady Cambridge herself. But what excuse could she find to call on a woman who that journalist had said was even more reclusive than the elusive Montgomery Flinch?

As Penelope stepped through the doors of the asylum and out into the wintry chill, a cunning smile slowly spread across her lips. The answer was staring her right in the face. She knew the person with the perfect reason to call on Lady Cambridge. All she needed to do now was convince him to agree.

XIII

"Absolutely not!"

Monty sat defiantly in the leather armchair, its shabby armrests stained in several places. "There's no way on earth I'm getting myself involved in that madness once again!"

Penelope sat primly on an armchair facing the actor, waiting patiently for his storm of protest to blow itself out. Monty swayed slightly in his seat, the last dregs of his brandy spilling out over the edge of his glass.

"The place was filled with crackpots and maniacs." Monty slurred his words as he jabbed a warning finger in Penelope's direction. "We were lucky to get out of there alive—you should be thanking me."

His cheeks shone with an intoxicated glow and, as his stentorian voice filled the club's saloon room, an elderly gentleman dozing in a nearby armchair woke with a start. The old man blinked, his eyes fixing on Penelope for a moment. Then, shaking his head in disgust at the sight of a young girl in his club, he fell back to sleep with an angry *harrumph*.

"I've already told you, Monty," Penelope spoke softly, her tone trying to soothe Monty's troubled countenance, "I don't want you to go back to Bedlam. You've just got to help me get inside Lady Cambridge's house."

Monty shook his head decisively.

"You hired me as an actor, my dear—someone to bring Montgomery Flinch's stories to life on the stage. Not as some sort of charlatan who would help you to prey on elderly members of the aristocracy."

Penelope frowned. "We wouldn't be preying on anyone—I'm just asking you to stick to your side of the bargain and play the part of Montgomery Flinch. Besides," she added, "at twenty-four years of age, I'd hardly call the widowed Lady Cambridge elderly."

At this morsel of information, Monty raised his eyebrow in interest.

"Twenty-four years old? Widowed, you say?"

Penelope nodded her head.

"So you'll come with me?"

There was a long moment of silence. The fingers of Monty's free hand drummed against the armrest as though considering the matter, but then, with a sigh, he shook his head again.

"No, no, no," he replied. "I refuse to be a part of this deception. No good will come of it, you mark my words."

Glancing up at the waiter standing unobtrusively in the corner of the room, he motioned for him to refill his glass.

The waiter glided across the threadbare carpet to Monty's side.

"Can I help you, sir?"

Monty brandished his empty glass.

"Another fine measure in there, my good man." He nodded benevolently in Penelope's direction. "And a drink for the young lady too—a lemonade perhaps—something to take the edge off her disappointment."

With an apologetic cough, the waiter slowly shook his head.

"I'm afraid that won't be possible, sir."

Monty looked up in surprise, his glowering face reddening to an even deeper hue.

"What do you mean 'won't be possible'?" he demanded. "Do you know how long I've been a member of this club?"

The young waiter nodded, his features composed in a sympathetic manner. "I do, sir," he replied, lowering his voice in deference to Penelope's presence, "but I have strict instructions from the club steward not to serve you with any more drinks until your subscriptions have been paid and the drinks bill settled in full."

"This is ridiculous," Monty blustered. "I'm only a couple of weeks in arrears."

"Three months, sir," the waiter replied. He reached down and took the empty glass from Monty's hand, placing it on his tray. "The steward can be found in his office if you would like to discuss the matter further with him."

Monty's face fell like a child who had unwrapped a brightly colored Christmas present and found only coal. He turned to Penelope for assistance.

"It's a trifling amount," he told her. "If you could just—"

Penelope rose to her feet, straightening her dress as she stood. "I'll see you tomorrow afternoon at two," she replied firmly. "The address is Stanley House, Two Egerton Gardens, South Kensington. I'll send a telegraph ahead so that Lady Cambridge is expecting our arrival."

With a mournful glance at his empty glass as the waiter bore it away, Monty slowly nodded his head.

Penelope turned and headed for the exit, her excitement mounting with every step that she took. Now she could start getting somewhere.

"I'll speak to the steward on my way out," she called back over her shoulder as the saloon doors closed behind her.

With Monty's money worries for the moment taken care of, Penelope stepped out of his club with a new spring in her step. Now she just had to head back to the offices of the *Penny Dreadful* to write the telegram that would gain their admittance into Lady Cambridge's home.

The fog that had clung to the streets since morning was clearing now, but Penelope's mind still swirled with questions. She was convinced that the key to unlocking this mystery lay with Lady Cambridge, but how exactly? Penelope was so absorbed in her thoughts that she didn't even notice the man walking in step beside her until he spoke.

"Been paying a visit to your uncle, Miss Tredwell?" the man inquired. "How is the illustrious Montgomery Flinch?"

Penelope's gaze swiveled in surprise and she found herself looking up into the face of the *Pall Mall Gazette's* inquisitive reporter, Mr. Robert Barrett.

"When you said he was staying at his country house residence," Barrett continued, casting a dismissive glance back at the worn façade of the gentlemen's club, "I was expecting somewhere a little more luxurious."

Penelope's mind raced as she quickened her step. How had Barrett found her here?

"Mr. Flinch was called back to London on urgent business," she replied, her mind struggling to keep pace with her mouth as she improvised desperately. "This gentlemen's club is his place of residence in the city while he attends to matters at the *Penny Dreadful.*"

Barrett raised an eyebrow as he quickened his step to keep pace with Penelope.

"I would have expected such a celebrated man of letters as Mr. Flinch to be a member of the Arts Club or the Athenaeum, not such a low-rent establishment as Rathbone's Club for Gentlemen of Leisure."

Penelope sharpened her smile in reply.

"I'm really not familiar with the merits of different gentlemen's clubs, Mr. Barrett," she quipped as she stepped smartly past a barrow being wheeled along the pavement.

"Of course, of course, it's unfair for me to ask a young lady such a question," said Barrett, holding his hands up in apology, as he dodged past the same barrow, "but there is just one small matter that I wonder if you could help me with."

At the end of the street, Penelope saw a row of hansom cabs waiting for a fare. With a sigh, she grudgingly nodded her assent. She'd soon be in a cab back to the *Penny Dreadful* and have this nosy journalist out of her hair.

"It's a puzzling trifle, but one that I'm sure you can explain," Barrett continued with an inquisitive gleam in his eye. "Why is Montgomery Flinch listed on the membership rolls at Rathbone's as a Mr. Monty Maples?"

Penelope stopped in her tracks, unable to hide

the panicked look that flashed across her face. She'd told Monty to cover his tracks. If Barrett pulled too firmly on this one loose thread, then the whole plan could unravel. Her secret would be out and the world would know the truth about Montgomery Flinch. She couldn't let that happen. Thinking on her feet, Penelope turned to face Barrett.

"You don't really think that a man of Montgomery Flinch's fame would be able to keep his privacy if he put his real name on the rolls of his club?" she replied, her lips pursed in a scornful half-smile. "He'd spend all his time signing autographs rather than writing the stories that have made his name. Now if that's all you wanted to ask me, Mr. Barrett, then I'll bid you good day."

Barrett frowned, but before he had the chance to reply, Penelope had already turned on her heel. As she hurried toward the line of horse-drawn cabs, her smile quickly turned to a scowl.

Penelope hailed the nearest hansom and clambered up into the cab before Barrett could follow her.

"The offices of the *Penny Dreadful*," she told the cabman. "Thirty-Eight Bedford Street, just off the Strand."

As the driver whipped his horses into life and the cab clattered across the cobbles, Penelope settled into her seat with a frown. Barrett's prying questions were getting too close for comfort. She needed to shake him off Montgomery Flinch's tail for good. Her fingers drummed against the seat's upholstery as her mind searched for a solution.

The answer came to her in an instant. When she got back to the office, she wouldn't just write a telegram to Lady Cambridge, but also one to Barrett's editor at the *Pall Mall Gazette*. It was time to give this pestering paper their exclusive interview with Montgomery Flinch, but on her terms. And that meant throwing this busybody journalist off the story and out of the picture. Otherwise, the *Gazette* could say good-bye forever to the pots of money the *Penny Dreadful* spent on advertising in its pages.

The cab driver turned into Trafalgar Square. From the window of the cab, Penelope could see Nelson's Column, the top of the towering monument still wreathed in mist. She sank back into her seat with a satisfied sigh. With Barrett out of the way, she'd be able to concentrate on solving the strange mystery that haunted Bedlam. Tomorrow she would pay a visit to Lady Cambridge and find out if she had any answers.

XIV

"Mr. Montgomery Flinch and his niece, Miss Penelope Tredwell, ma'am."

The stiff-necked butler ushered them through a set of double doors into a cavernous drawing room. Penelope stifled a gasp as she entered the room. Outside, the wintry gloom was already darkening the windows, but the room itself was uncommonly bright. It was lit by an array of incandescent electric lamps that hung from the ceiling in glowing globes. Penelope felt her feet sink into the velvet-pile carpet. Penelope's gaze darted around the room, quickly taking in her surroundings with an author's eye.

In one corner of the room, a grand piano stood silent, its polished ebony-black veneer shining beneath the lamplight. Elsewhere, luxurious chairs and couches, tables, and chiffoniers were elegantly arranged around the room. Wealth dripped from every surface. The back wall was filled entirely by a vast bookcase which stretched from floor to ceiling, its shelves crammed with rows of leather-bound volumes. On the remaining walls, the shimmering black-and-white patterned threads of the wallpaper made Penelope feel as though she were trapped in a spider's web.

Rising from her armchair, Lady Cambridge stepped forward to greet them. She was dressed in a flowing black gown, widow's weeds that made mourning look distinctly fashionable. Dark waves of hair were artfully swept up to the top of her head and her pale face was illuminated by a pair of blue eyes, sparkling with a bewitching beauty. Penelope heard Monty sharply draw his breath in awe, captivated by the widow's youthful allure.

"Mr. Flinch, what an unexpected delight to meet you." Lady Cambridge took Monty's hand in a delicate handshake. "My staff inform me that your stories are all the rage in literary London."

"Why—thank you," Monty replied, stumbling over his words like a nervous schoolboy. "I'm so honored, my lady, that you have even heard of my trifling serials."

Her own outstretched hand ignored, Penelope tried to bite her lip but couldn't stop herself asking the question.

"You've not read any of my uncle's stories yourself then?"

Lady Cambridge turned to look down at Penelope, a faint air of amusement playing across her features. “I must admit I haven’t,” she confided, her lips curling in a gently mocking smile. “I prefer to deal in fact rather than fictions.”

She turned away, motioning for them both to take a seat as she returned to her own chair. “Your telegram said that you wanted to consult me for my expertise, Mr. Flinch. Pray tell me, how exactly can I help you?”

Monty stayed rooted to the spot, watching Lady Cambridge with a bedazzled expression on his face as she swished her way back to her chair.

“Telegram?” he replied distractedly.

Penelope swiftly brought the heel of her boot down on the actor’s foot to jolt him out of his enchantment.

“Ouch!”

Arranging herself in her chair, Lady Cambridge glanced up in surprise at Monty’s sudden exclamation.

Grimacing, he raised his hand in apology. “I’m sorry—old war wound. It plays me up from time to time.”

Monty hobbled toward the pair of vacant armchairs, snatching an angry glance at Penelope as she sat down beside him.

Lady Cambridge stared coolly at the two of them, a flicker of suspicion in her gaze. “So what little knowledge of mine do you wish to avail yourself of, Mr. Flinch?” she asked pointedly.

“Ah yes,” said Monty, gathering himself

together. "I wish to question you on your expert knowledge of all things arachnid."

At these words, Penelope saw Lady Cambridge's hands grasp the arms of her chair, her slender fingers whitening with the pressure of her grip. Unaware of this, Monty blithely carried on speaking. His words had a slightly over-rehearsed quality to them, as though this was a speech he had been practicing.

"As you know, my dear Lady, in the past year I have built a towering reputation as the author of many bestselling serials. My stories are chilling tales of mystery, intricately plotted episodes for the reading public to puzzle over. Of late, I have had the beginnings of a new tale start to take shape in my mind—a diabolical mystery whose plot hinges on the perfect murder." Monty paused, a conceited smirk playing across his lips. "Of course, I have disregarded all the conventional methods of murder: the revolver, the dagger, the rope, the lead piping. These are all too plain for my tale and my readers expect to be intrigued."

"I really don't see how I can—"

Monty cut off Lady Cambridge's interruption with a reassuring wave of his hand. "I was thinking of the bite of a deadly spider—a venomous poison undetectable by human hand but that could polish off its victim in a matter of seconds. I wondered, Lady Cambridge, whether you would be able to suggest a suitable species of spider to ensure the essential truthfulness of my tale?"

Lady Cambridge's lips tightened, the sudden hardening of her face marring its perfect beauty. She stared at Monty, an angry gleam in her dark-blue eyes. "I don't believe I can help you, Mr. Flinch," she replied coldly. "My studies of the spider have been to further mankind's understanding of these remarkable creatures, not to make them the tool of some pantomime villain in a tawdry shilling shocker."

Monty was taken aback by Lady Cambridge's swift change of mood. "I can assure you, my lady," he spluttered, "this tale would be no shilling shocker. The *Penny Dreadful* is a highly respected periodical read by doctors, lawyers, even ministers of state. The sales of our latest issue are nearing a million. Your assistance in this matter would be of immeasurable service to the cause of great literature."

In spite of Monty's flattery, Lady Cambridge sat impassive on her chair. The cold beauty of her face set firm against any persuasion.

"You have had my answer, Mr. Flinch." She reached down to the small rosewood table beside her and lifted the bell there. She rang it with an imperious wave of her hand. "I would thank you not to call again. Good day to you both."

From a side door, the butler noiselessly entered the drawing room. With a respectful beckoning motion, he hurriedly ushered them from the room, Monty still indignantly protesting that his intentions had been misunderstood. As the double doors slowly closed behind them, Penelope glanced back over her shoulder. For a moment, her eyes met Lady Cambridge's and a chill ran down Penelope's spine as she saw the malice in her gaze. Then the doors shut with a noise like a pistol crack.

The butler swept them down the long entrance hall, foisting their coats into their arms and then depositing Monty and Penelope on the stone steps outside. The front door closed behind them with a slam.

"Well, that was a waste of time," said Monty bitterly, pulling up the collar of his overcoat as an icy sleet began to fall from the fog-bound sky.

Penelope stood in silence on the rain-splattered steps, her face clouded in suspicion. Behind her green eyes, her mind worked frantically to try to unravel what had just taken place. Monty's cover story about the spiders had just been a bluff to get them through the door, but Lady Cambridge's reaction to it had been so extreme. Was there something else at play here? Something that she was missing? Whatever it might be, not a trace of doubt remained in her mind that Lady Cambridge had something to hide.

She glanced up at Monty, her eyes shining with a fierce determination.

"I found out what I needed to know."

Alone in the drawing room, Lady Cambridge slowly rose from her chair. Reaching for the light switch, she dimmed the lamps and then stepped toward the back wall and the towering bookcase that loomed there. Running a manicured hand along one of its shelves, she spoke softly to herself, her words almost lost in the cavernous hush.

"What a vulgar little man," she murmured. "How on earth could he imagine that I would use you, my darlings, to help him write his catchpenny potboiler?"

Her hand trailed past the leather-bound volumes and buffed ornaments set upon on the shelf, her finger catching against one of the curios with an audible click.

The bookshelves began to slide noiselessly back, gliding apart to reveal the darkness hidden behind. Lady Cambridge stepped out of the drawing room and into what looked like a jungle. Towering branches and ferns arched skyward behind a glass screen, lit from within by a strange blue-tinted glow. A skein of sticky webs hung from every surface; some were messy jumbles of gossamer threads hanging like hammocks between leaves and branches, others, delicately spun circles of silk strung across the ferns. It was a vast vivarium filled with countless scurrying spiders of every size and every color.

From an overhanging branch, a snaking stream of tiny spiderlings spilled out from a bulbous cocoon, clambering up the mossy limb and out across the shrouding leaves. In the shadows beneath these, the corpse of a mummified mouse lay wrapped in a silken shroud as a giant tarantula crawled greedily toward it. Behind the glass, every inch of the spidertorium was crawling with arachnid life.

Lady Cambridge rested her head against the glass, staring into the pale blue mists that clung to the ferns and branches.

"You are destined for a much higher purpose," she purred, as the spiders scurried to and fro before her eyes. "We're almost there. Soon, all will be revealed."

XV

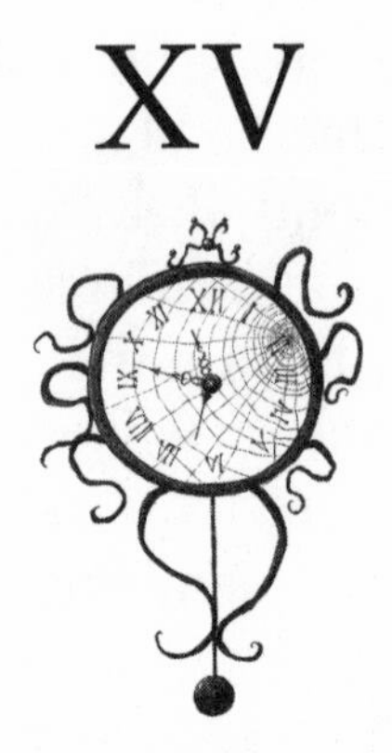

The drawing room lay in darkness, the vast bookcase now back in position along the far wall. Through a crack in the curtains, a slender shaft of moonlight illuminated the door as it softly swung open. A slight black-coated figure crept into the room like a thief, pausing with every footstep as the tick of the grandfather clock standing in the corner kept time with her thumping heartbeat.

Penelope glanced around the room, its furnishings now shrouded in shadows. As she moved forward, her leg brushed against a corner table and she quickly had to reach out to right a glass vase as it teetered precariously. She could barely see more than a few inches in front of her face, but she couldn't risk turning the lights on. The danger of discovery was too great.

So far everything had gone to plan. The master key in her pocket had opened every locked door that Penelope had encountered. It had been a delicate operation to acquire the key, her light fingers surreptitiously lifting it from the loop of keys on the butler's belt as he had handed her back her coat earlier that day. As they had been bustled out of the front door, she had scanned the servants' roster lying on the hall table by the entrance and had carefully noted the number of servants on duty that night, registering the manner of their duties and the hour by which they retired. From this information, it had just been a case of timing her return, sneaking in through the servants' entrance as the clocks rang two.

Penelope edged her way forward, taking care not to trip over any of the furniture as she crept through the darkness. As she reached the far end of the room, the sheer cliff face of the bookcase rose up in front of her, blocking her path completely. She shook her head in puzzlement. As well as the master key, Penelope had the carefully folded plans to the house tucked into her pocket. She had obtained these from the Land Registry offices that very afternoon, bribing the clerk there with a signed copy of the latest *Penny Dreadful*. According to these plans there should be a set of steps to a whole other room here, a chambered vault spanning the width of the house.

She walked the length of the wall, her hand trailing along the bookshelves for guidance. Perplexed, Penelope reached inside the pocket of her overcoat, drawing out the plans with one hand, while with her other she fumbled free a box of matches.

Spreading the plans out across a shelf, she sparked one of the matches into life, its phosphorescent glow casting an eerie light across the architect blueprints. Penelope could see the drawing room clearly marked on the plans and beyond this, steps leading down to a basement space. She glanced back along the bookcase as the flame guttered and died. There were no steps here.

Penelope frowned as she folded the plans, carefully returning them to her pocket as she puzzled over this enigma. Casting a nervous glance toward the door, she struck another match, its flickering flame warm against her face in the frigid air. She leaned in more closely to inspect the bookcase, its solid oak shelves giving every impression of having stood there forever and a day. The flame of the match illuminated the books lining the shelves, their titles spelled out in shining gold letters across their spines: *The Natural History of the Arachnid, The Spiders of South America, Journals of the British Empire Arachnological Society*. No trace of Montgomery Flinch's fictions or the pages of the *Penny Dreadful* anywhere on these shelves.

Penelope bristled at the recollection of Lady Cambridge's dismissal of her stories as tawdry shilling shockers. The shadows cast by the flickering flame of the dying match danced across the bookcase. If this was some shilling shocker, she mused, then there would be a secret entrance to the basement hidden somewhere behind this. As the flame died away, she quickly lit another match and then reaching out with her free hand, ran her fingers along the underside of the bookshelf, searching for some kind of hidden button or catch. She sighed in disappointment; there was nothing there.

Then Penelope heard the faint sound of a click, and from beneath the door to the drawing room a warm pool of light spilled out. The sound of footsteps and two female voices grew louder as electric lamps glowed in the hall outside. Panicking, Penelope quickly turned to hide, her eyes frantically searching the room for a place of safety. She darted toward the window curtains, but as she turned, her foot snagged on the edge of a rug, pitching her forward with a startled gasp.

Flinging out an arm to save herself, Penelope's hand caught hold of an ornament on the bookcase. The figurine tipped as she fell, catching with a click as she sank to her knees in the shadow of the bookcase. Then, with a hushed whir, the bookshelves slowly began to slide apart and Penelope stared up in disbelief into a darkened jungle. She could see ferns and creepers twisting toward the ceiling as night-blooming flowers unfurled their petals behind the glass. Twining branches hung heavy with silken webs, every inch of their bark swarming with spiders.

Leaning closer in wonderment, Penelope watched as a fly blundered into a loose spiral of spider's web, captured in its shining strands of stickiness. At the heart of the web, a large black spider sat motionless, waiting patiently as the fly twitched and struggled, the captured insect only succeeding in binding itself more tightly in the spider's trap. Despite the warmth of her coat, Penelope shivered. She watched as the spider skittered across the web, stealthily moving closer to the fly.

A sudden clatter of footsteps outside brought Penelope back to her senses. Quickly rising to her feet, she glimpsed a darkened set of steps to the left of the vast glass case. The plans had been right after all! Stepping to her left, she righted the figurine on the bookcase, the ornament snapping back into position with a click, and the shelves began to slide shut once more. Penelope darted through the narrowing gap and down the steps into the darkness as they closed completely behind her.

As she stood there alone in the blackness, Penelope heard the muffled sound of voices and footsteps. Her heart thudded in her chest, the noise of it almost drowning the soft murmur of voices on the other side of the bookcase. Penelope strained her ears to make out the words.

"—I don't see why we should have to prepare rooms to entertain visitors at a time when all decent folk are in bed. It's not proper."

The muffled grumble of the woman's voice was cut off by a sharp shushing sound.

"Hush," a second voice warned. "Don't let Her ladyship catch you saying those things. Not unless you want to find yourself out on the street."

The fear in the woman's voice was obvious to Penelope, even as the bookcase between them muffled the sound. Standing frozen in the darkness, Penelope breathed with slow silent breaths, frightened that any movement would alert the servants to her presence. The blackness surrounded her, solid as a wall pressing against her face, but slowly her eyes began to get used to the darkness. She could make out a soft glow in the gloom, the twisted shape of a branch coated with a phosphorescent moss. And crawling across this, the silhouette shape of a black widow spider only inches from her face.

Penelope stumbled backward, her footsteps clattering down the steps as the bustling noise from the servants above slowly moved away. Breathing heavily, she froze, terrified that she had been overheard. She listened intently, but there was no answering sound from the room above. The servants had gone.

Glancing down, Penelope saw a soft orange light spilling up from the bottom of the steps on which she was standing. Moving as noiselessly as she could, she left the spiders scurrying beneath the glass behind and retreated down the steps in search of the hidden room below. Reaching the bottom of the steps, Penelope looked around to see a spacious chamber, dimly lit by a handful of yellow bulbs that hung down from the ceiling, each half-covered with a broad metal shade.

The basement seemed to extend endlessly back into the gloom. Penelope saw several rows of tall wooden cabinets, arranged at regular intervals between the oak-paneled walls, with narrow aisles leading between them. In front of the cabinets were two plush easy chairs set beside a long, low table covered with scattered papers.

Penelope walked over to the table and reached down to gather up one of the pages that lay abandoned there. The spidery scrawl of the handwriting told her what she had already suspected. This was where Bradburn had brought the Midnight Papers. She peered more closely at the sheet, trying to decipher the words scratched across it.

...an electronic eye staring out into every room...BBC, MTV, CCTV...the watched and the watchers...flickering pictures beamed across the globe in an instant...thousands of channels filled with the babblings of fools...all must obey the remote control...

The same unsettling certainty she had seen in the other patients' writings haunted these words, but the meaning of them was lost in the minds of the Bedlamites. Placing the paper back on the table, Penelope moved toward the nearest row of cabinets. Lady Cambridge had stolen these papers for a reason and Penelope was determined to find out why.

Under the glare of the dim yellow bulb hanging overhead, the golden grain of the oak cabinet glowed slightly. The narrow filing cabinet was fronted by nine drawers, each with a brass handle and a name holder above it. Penelope pulled out the drawer at the level of her waist, the printed label reading *1903*. The drawer rolled open to reveal a stack of index cards, disappearing back into the depths of the cabinet. It looked like some kind of library catalog. Penelope drew out a card from the crowded drawer. Bringing it into the light, she saw clipped fragments of the patients' writings, carefully pasted onto the card.

> *...with twin propellers, man launches into the sky on slender wings...Orville and Wilbur Wright, pilots of the future...at Kitty Hawk, North Carolina, the Flyer soars...*

Beneath the patients' scribbled handwriting, a neater, more controlled hand had printed the following comment:

The invention of heavier-than-air flight? Track down the Wright brothers to investigate further.

Mystified, Penelope leafed through the other cards in the file. More fragments from the Midnight Papers were found on each one, the meaning behind the patients' words still evading her understanding. But on each card, the same neat hand as before had printed an accompanying commentary.

Britain takes over the Fulani Empire—Lord Salisbury dies—Edward VII proclaimed Emperor of India

Shaking her head in confusion, Penelope placed the cards back into the stack and slid the drawer closed. She moved along the row of cabinets, pulling drawers open at random, each with a different number printed across the name holder: 1917, 1939, 1966, 1997, 2001. Penelope flicked through the cards, trying to piece the mystery together. On each one, the patients' fantastical visions were translated into cold hard statements of fact.

As she reached the end of the row, Penelope turned and stared back along the cabinets, her mind whirring with questions. She glanced down at the last card in her hand, an ominous prophecy that chilled her blood.

Great iron birds fall from the sky on the Empire State...nations weep as the twin towers fall...

New York attacked—America at war.

Standing there in the gloom, Penelope realized for the first time that the numbers in the name holders had been rising with every step she took. From 1900 to 2001, each of the labels matched a year from the twentieth century to come and beyond. With a sudden gasp of revelation, she understood what the patients' writings were. Their visions were visions of the future, predictions of a time yet to come.

Lost in thought, Penelope didn't hear the sound of footsteps until they had almost reached the bottom of the stairs. The caustic tones of Lady Cambridge's voice echoed across the subterranean chamber.

"I do hope you have a good reason for disturbing me at this hour of the night."

XVI

Penelope scrambled backward, the heel of her boot scraping against the wooden floorboards. Wrapping herself in the darkness of her coat, she crouched behind the farthest of the filing cabinets, sheltering in its shadow as the footsteps entered the room. The echo of Lady Cambridge's voice was followed by the heavier tread of a second set of footsteps, and Penelope held her breath in fear. Then she heard the low rumble of Bradburn's voice answer in reply.

"I had no choice—I had to come."

Peering around the edge of the filing cabinet, Penelope saw the statuesque figure of Lady Cambridge standing imperiously beside the table and chairs at the front of the chamber. She was dressed in a white linen nightdress and shawl, the lace-trimmed material flowing from her neck to her toes, but the stark beauty of her features was marred by a thunderous look. Facing her,

Bradburn wrung his grimy cap in his hands, the scar-faced orderly shifting uncomfortably beneath her gaze.

"No choice?" Lady Cambridge replied sharply. "No choice but to go against all our carefully planned arrangements? No choice but to raise me from my bed at this ungodly hour? May I remind you, Mr. Bradburn, that I am a recently widowed Lady of unblemished reputation. If anyone should have seen you sullying my doorstep—"

"I promise you, Lady Cambridge," Bradburn protested, "nobody saw me."

"My servants saw you," Lady Cambridge snapped in reply. "Servants see, servants talk. I keep my staff firmly in line here, but even they raise an eyebrow when some guttersnipe arrives on my doorstep at half past two in the morning.

"And what for?" she continued, brandishing a thin sheaf of papers. "This?"

Even through the gloom, Penelope could just make out the familiar spidery scrawls scratched across the topmost sheet.

"There are hundreds of patients in Bedlam, yet tonight you've brought me the work of only a handful of them." Lady Cambridge flung the papers down on the table and turned on the orderly with a snarl. "What exactly am I paying you for?"

Bradburn scowled as the pages scattered in front of him.

"This was all I could smuggle away," he muttered in a guttural growl. "It's not like when I could just sneak the papers out one night at a time and put the ones you didn't need back the next day. Ever since that blasted author Flinch came sniffing around, Bedlam's been tight as a drum. Dr. Morris is collecting the papers from the cells almost as soon as the freaks finish writing them."

Listening from the shadows, Penelope felt a nervous thrill of excitement. It seemed that she had already managed to throw a wrench into the workings of Lady Cambridge's mysterious plan.

"It's not good enough," Lady Cambridge replied, a hard edge of steel entering her words. "For six long months I have labored at this scheme and only a handful of years are yet to be revealed. The days of the nineteenth century are almost at an end—I need those papers." She pointed toward the shadowy rows of oak cabinets, her lace-trimmed sleeve draped decorously from her arm. "When the last pieces of the jigsaw are in place, the course of the coming century will be determined by me. I will hold the secrets of all the wonders and the horrors yet to come. The fate of nations, the entire world will rest in my hands." Her dark blue eyes flashed in warning. "You would do well not to disappoint me, Mr. Bradburn."

"But what can I do?" the truculent orderly moaned. "They've got the nurses running double shifts at midnight now—they're watching the patients like hawks. I can barely slip them their nightly dose without getting caught. How am I supposed to get more of the Midnight Papers out of there?"

A cunning smile slowly crept across Lady Cambridge's lips. "We just need to change the time you administer the dose," she replied, "so it takes hold when there won't be as many people on guard. There's no need for us to wait until twelve minutes to midnight to find out what the future holds."

Tossing her hair back decisively, she strode toward a walnut cabinet at the far end of the room. Craning her neck to follow her path, Penelope edged out of the shadows. She noticed for the first time that this cabinet wasn't a filing cabinet like all the others, but instead a medicine cabinet with rows of jars and bottles neatly arranged on shelves behind a glass door. Opening the door, Lady Cambridge drew out a tray filled with tiny glass vials and turned to face Bradburn.

"You go back to Bedlam now," she told him. "Administer a double dose to every patient."

The orderly blanched, the color draining from his face in an instant.

"But the last time I gave them all a double dose, one of the inmates died," he protested. "If that happens again and I'm caught, they'll string me up for murder."

Lady Cambridge was unmoved. "We've no time left to waste," she told him. "Before the dawn rises,

I want you to bring me back the final dispatches from the century to come."

She thrust the tray toward him and, with apelike fingers, Bradburn clumsily reached for the glass vials. He transferred them, one by one, from the tray to the folds of his overcoat pocket. As he worked, Penelope crept forward in the gloom. Reaching the end of the row, she rested her hand against a shadowy filing cabinet and peered around it. She had to find out what was in those vials. The cloudy liquid inside each one shimmered like tiny teardrops as the glass vials clinked into place.

Penelope felt a prickling sensation on the back of her hand. Glancing down, she saw, with a sudden rush of horror, a large red-and-black spider crawling across her skin. As she flung out her hand in fear, its pointed fangs struck out, piercing her skin and pumping their venom in. A low moan escaped from Penelope's lips, the pain from the bite impossible to contain. Landing on the ground, the spider scurried back into the shadows, while Penelope stood there swaying, her hand clinging to the cabinet for support.

With a cold sweat soaking her brow, Penelope could feel her muscles begin to twitch in spasm as the venom took hold. It felt as though a huge weight was pressing down on her from within. Her breath came in shallow juddering gasps as a creeping paralysis began to crawl through her veins. Penelope could feel her arms, legs, even the muscles in her face stiffening as the poison spread. She tried to shuffle backward, desperate to take refuge in the shadows until the feeling had passed, but her feet wouldn't obey and she tumbled to the floor with a crash.

"What in damnation was that?"

Bradburn's bark echoed through the basement. Frozen where she lay, Penelope stared up helplessly as hurried footsteps approached. Lady Cambridge and the orderly stood over her.

"It's that girl who was snooping around the hospital with Flinch," Bradburn snarled. "That damned author must be around here somewhere."

Casting her cold eyes along the shadowy row of cabinets, Lady Cambridge shook her head. She stared down at Penelope, an unsettling smile fixed upon her face.

"I think the girl has come alone. Miss Tredwell, isn't it?"

Penelope could only nod her head mutely as the freezing paralysis crept across her lips. She watched with a growing sense of dread as the same large spider crawled down Lady Cambridge's arm. Silhouetted against the sleeve of the cotton nightdress, its shiny black body was split by bloodred stripes. As the burly orderly edged away in revulsion, Lady Cambridge stood there unmoved, the spider finally nestling in the hollow of her open palm.

"*Latrodectus torperus*," she declared, stroking a

finger along the back of the spider. "A rare arachnid of the black widow genus. You have nothing to be scared of, my dear," she told Penelope, leaning down to place a soothing hand on her feverish scalp. "Its bite is not fatal and the effects wear off in a matter of hours. Its venom merely induces a fast-acting paralysis, numbing the nerves and muscles until its victims cannot move an inch. So much more effective than a guard dog, I find."

A worried look flashed across Bradburn's face.

"If she's not going to kick the bucket then how are we going to get rid of her?" he asked gruffly.

Lady Cambridge took a step toward him, the spider still held in her palm. As the orderly tried to pull back, she reached into his pocket and withdrew one of the glass vials.

"Take her back to Bedlam with you," she ordered as Bradburn's scarred face flushed with relief. "A triple dose should be enough to tip her into madness. That will be the last we hear of Miss Penelope Tredwell."

Kneeling down on the floor beside Penelope, Lady Cambridge pulled the stopper from the neck of the vial. Inside the glass, the cloudy liquid swirled in the gloomy half-light.

"In some ways I envy you," she told Penelope, as she prepared to pour the liquid into her mouth. "The dreams you will have, the wonders you will see."

Her mind trapped behind an expressionless

mask, Penelope's thoughts raced in fear. She had finally discovered who was behind the sinister events at Bedlam, just in time to be dragged into the heart of the nightmare herself. As Lady Cambridge bent closer, the glinting vial held in her hand, Penelope struggled to free herself. Every inch of her body trembled as she tried to escape, but the freezing paralysis held her tightly in its grasp. She strained to force a few words from her lips, desperate to ask the one question left in this mystery.

"What is it?" she hissed through gritted teeth.

Lady Cambridge raised an eyebrow in surprise.

"My dear, you do have a hardy constitution for one so young," she replied, the vial poised in midair. "This is the venom of a creature long-thought extinct. *Architarbi somnerus*—the dream-weaver spider. I discovered it in the depths of Africa. My husband and I encountered a remote tribe in Abyssinia who hunted and captured the spiders alive. Their medicine man extracted the venom and used it in the primitive ceremonies they're so fond of over there. He claimed to us that drinking the venom brought him visions of the tribe's future. He said that he had prophesied that we would come—that he had seen us before in his dreams and knew the fates that would befall us."

Lady Cambridge stared down at Penelope, the certainty of her smile suddenly chilling.

"The medicine man told me that the spiders

had been waiting for me—the woman who would weave their webs around the world. The Spider Lady—the keeper of their secrets. All I had to do was harvest from the minds of men the visions that the spiders' venom revealed. Then I would wield a power greater than anyone had ever known. The future itself would be mine to tell."

She paused for a moment as if reliving the memory.

"But the tribesman told me something else too," Lady Cambridge confided, her eyes narrowing as she spoke. "He said that the spiders were dying out; the strange powers they held waning as the century drew to a close. He warned me that if I did not fulfil this prophecy by the day the twentieth century dawned, then the spiders would betray me and snare me forever in a nightmare. I only have until this New Year's Eve to seize my destiny."

The thin line of Lady Cambridge's smile hardened. "My husband thought this was all mumbo-jumbo, especially when the medicine man warned him that he would never leave the shores of Africa alive." Her eyes glittered darkly. "He sadly passed away soon after this, but I brought a colony of dream-weaver spiders back with me to England. With these creatures at my command, I could read the pages of history before they were even written. There was only one drawback—anyone who drank the venom of the dream-maker spider was driven into the arms of madness. It seems that the constitutions of our fellow countrymen are not as resilient as those of the Abyssinian tribesmen." She glanced up at Bradburn, the orderly still staring nervously at the black widow spider crouching in the shadows by her side. "So who better to bring me news of the world yet to come than those who are already mad?"

As the vial hovered over her lips, Penelope found the strength to whisper a final question.

"Why?"

Lady Cambridge shook her head scornfully as though she couldn't believe Penelope's foolishness.

"We stand on the brink of a brand-new century—the last of the millennium. Why should we peer only inches into the future when we could see for miles? Soon, kings, queens, prime ministers, and presidents will kneel at my feet to learn the secrets I hold. I can sell this knowledge to the highest bidder—even change the course of history with one touch of the tiller."

She tipped her hand, forcing the open vial between Penelope's lips. "Now drink up, my dear," she said with a terrible smile. "I want you to tell me my future."

Penelope gagged as the foul-tasting liquid slipped down her throat, but Lady Cambridge kept the vial pressed tightly to her lips until every last drop was swallowed.

"There, there," she breathed with a satisfied sigh. "Time to sleep, perchance to dream."

Penelope lay there frozen, unable to respond. Lady Cambridge's voice echoed strangely in her mind, the words sounding as though they were coming from a great distance away. She watched powerlessly as Lady Cambridge rose to her feet, gathering her white shawl around her and turning toward Bradburn.

"Now get her back to Bedlam and bring me those papers."

Penelope could feel her eyelids growing heavy, a darkness crowding in on all sides as the venom flowed through her veins. Her brain itched with the scurrying of a thousand tiny legs; her mind crawling with spiders. As the darkness overwhelmed her, the last thing Penelope saw was Bradburn's twisted face leaning closer, his monstrous hands reaching toward her.

XVII

Thick fog clung to the streets outside, dimming the light from the electric streetlamps to a feeble glow. There was a frost in the air and heavy clouds scudded across the blackness of the sky. Alfie sheltered in the shadow of the grand house, his hands thrust deep into his jacket pockets against the chill. He peered anxiously into the gloom, his eyes fixed on the servants' entrance that sheltered beneath the broad stone steps that led to the front door.

Penelope had said she'd only be in there for ten minutes—that was half an hour ago. Why had he let her talk him into this? It had been a lark following Bradburn through the streets of the city, hiding behind corners as he kept on his trail, but this was something else. This was breaking and entering—and the home of a lady to boot! If they got caught it would be the reform school for the both of them or even worse.

Alfie frowned. He had to go and get Penelope out of there before she got them into real trouble. He took two steps forward, but then pressed himself against the wall as the sound of horses' hooves and grating wheels clattered in the street outside. Glancing up in fear, Alfie peered into the darkness. Through a gap in the hedge, he saw a horse-drawn buggy come to a halt at the front of the house.

He watched as the lone driver swung down from the high seat. For a moment, the burly man was framed in silhouette beneath a streetlamp as he gathered together the two horses' reins to tether them there. Then he turned toward the house and Alfie saw Bradburn's grim features glaring at him through the gloom.

Alfie shrank back in the shadows, praying that the scar-faced orderly hadn't seen him there. Squinting through the fog, he watched Bradburn push open the front gate and then bound up the stone steps that led to the front door. The orderly rapped twice on the knocker, his second knock answered by a light inside. His heart pounding in his chest, Alfie glanced back at the servants' entrance, but the door there stayed firmly closed.

"Penny, where are you?" he whispered beneath his breath.

Alfie heard the sound of the front door opening, and, half-turning, he saw Bradburn disappear inside. The door closed behind the orderly with a slam, the sudden noise unnaturally loud in the silence of the night. With mounting horror, Alfie watched as behind heavy curtains the lights in the house came on one by one. From the entrance hall to the drawing room, the tall windows stared out like dimly lit eyes.

Alfie was torn. There was no way he could try and get inside with what looked like half the house awake now. But with Bradburn on the scene, Penelope was in real danger. He could only pray that she had found a place to hide. As a chill wind whipped around the side of the building, black thoughts raced through Alfie's brain.

He wasn't sure how long he stood there for, half frozen between action and despair, when the sound of a door opening jerked his gaze back to the front of the house. Alfie saw Bradburn hurrying down the stone steps, a heavy bundle wrapped in a cloak slung across his shoulder. Pushing the gate open, the burly orderly stepped out into the street. As he approached the open carriage, the two horses pawed the ground nervously.

Ignoring their whinnies, Bradburn hoisted the body-shaped bundle into the high seat of the buggy. As the brute turned to free the horses' reins, Alfie saw the cloak slip from the face of the shrouded form. He gasped with horror as through wreaths of mist he saw Penelope's face, her features deathly pale. Before Alfie could even decide what to do, Bradburn had clambered up into the seat next to Penelope.

"Come on, my girl," he growled. "Let's get you back to the madhouse."

With a snarl, he snapped the whip above the horses' heads and they set off at a gallop down the fog-bound street. Alfie raced to the gate as he watched the wheels of the carriage disappear into the mist. The sound of the horses' hooves slowly faded into silence, taking all trace of Penelope with them. What had they done to her?

Penelope felt herself lifted through the air, her numbed body dangling loosely from the orderly's arms. She couldn't tell where she was being taken, her senses disorientated as the spiders in her mind began to spin their webs. Seconds became minutes, minutes bled into hours. Alone in the darkness, time had no meaning. Fragments of feeling broke free through the fog: a biting wind whipping across her face, the clatter of horses' hooves and the babbling of voices. *Let's get you to the madhouse.*

Penelope tried to cling on to these memories as the venom crept through her veins. They were the only things keeping her anchored to the real world as her mind slowly slipped away. She could feel herself teetering on the edge of a vast abyss—an infinite darkness crisscrossed with countless black silken threads. Penelope knew that if she fell, she would be gone forever.

Fighting to keep her thoughts from the precipice, Penelope felt herself lifted again. Rough hands grappled her to the ground, the cloak that had shrouded her falling away. Penelope heard a rattle of keys and the slamming of doors and then she was dragged forward again, her legs scraping against the cold stone.

"Another one for the padded cells."

The growl of Bradburn's voice cut through her mind like a knife. Penelope struggled to free herself, but her limbs were frozen, useless. She felt herself pitched forward, her face sliding painfully against a polished floor as a second voice whined in reply.

"You can't bring her in here without the proper documents. What are you trying to do? Get me the sack?"

Penelope's eyelids flickered open; the only part of her body that seemed able to answer the desperate pleas that her brain was sending. On the edge of her vision she could see Bradburn arguing with a second orderly, a pimply-faced youth who quailed beneath the older guard's prodding finger. However, as Penelope's eyes focused straight ahead, she saw the worn mask of a woman's face staring back at her.

The woman was staring through the bars of her cell, a tiny window that revealed a half- shadowed glance of her wrinkled features. Dark green eyes peered down at Penelope with a pitying gaze. Her face looked strangely familiar, and Penelope tried to dredge the memory from the darkness of her mind. It was the patient who had stopped her in the corridors of Bedlam; the old-young woman with strange messages scratched across her skin.

Penelope tried to speak, her numbed lips struggling to shape the words. "Help me," she whispered.

The woman's worn face creased in a bitter smile, revealing again the blackened stumps of her teeth.

"It's no good asking for help," she hissed in reply. "Nobody listens. You're one of us now."

She flinched away from the window with a shriek as Bradburn slammed his open palm against the door of her cell.

"Be quiet!" he roared.

Then Bradburn turned, reaching down toward Penelope with menacing hands. The second orderly had unlocked the door of the adjacent cell and Bradburn dragged Penelope through this. In the dim light she could see the shadowy shapes of words stretching from the floor to the ceiling, looping whirls of black ink and bloodstains scratched across the walls. A renewed sense of panic rose in Penelope's chest. This was Fitzgerald's cell—the patient who had died only days before.

The burly orderly roughly laid her down on the cold, hard floor. Penelope tried to move, her fingers twitching as the paralysis started to weaken, but then Bradburn grabbed hold of her face. With cruel fingers, he forced her mouth open, pressing the hard-edged rim of the glass vial to her lips. His voice rasped in her ear.

"So you're still awake, are you?" he growled. "Well, a triple dose of this will soon send you off to dreamland with the rest of the blighters in here."

The vile liquid slicked into her mouth, a trickle of it spilling from her lips and dripping down onto the cold, stone floor of the asylum cell. Inside Penelope's mind, the spiders gathering there seethed in delight.

As Bradburn turned away, slamming the door of the cell shut behind him, the spiders' frenzied spinning began to draw Penelope inexorably toward the edge of the precipice. Beneath this, the shimmering darkness of a vast silken web shivered in anticipation, waiting for her to fall.

Monty muttered fearfully beneath his breath, the dark corridors of his dreams swiftly turning into a labyrinth. He ran without thought, blundering into the shadows as, all around him, a bedlam of voices called out his name. A hand grabbed at his shoulder and Monty turned in horror to find himself staring into the face of a nightmare.

"Mr. Maples! Mr. Maples!"

Monty woke with a spluttering start.

"What! What!"

The club steward stepped back in surprise. Around them in the saloon-room, the slumped shapes of a dozen sleeping forms shifted uneasily in their armchairs. In the dim light, Monty's last drink lay half-finished on the table beside him.

"What is it?" he slurred as he rubbed the sleep from his eyes.

"This young gentleman said that he needed to see you urgently," the steward replied, studiously ignoring the thin line of drool hanging from Monty's chin. "I told him that the club could not admit visitors at so late an hour, but he was most insistent."

Glancing up, Monty's gaze focused for the first time on Alfie, who was hovering anxiously behind the steward's shoulder.

"You've got to come with me, Monty!" Alfie cried out, forgetting the sober decorum of his surroundings as his impatience overtook him. "There's no way I can get into Bedlam without you."

Monty recoiled in horror, the thoughts of his nightmare still fresh in his mind.

"What on earth do you mean?" he stuttered. "Why would we want to go there?"

"To find Penny," Alfie replied, his eyes shining with fear, "before it's too late."

Lying on the cold, stone floor of the cell, Penelope gagged as the vile liquid swilled around her mouth. The taste of the venom burned her tongue, a tiny trickle of it slipping down her throat. Inside her mind, she felt the black silken threads of the web tighten their grip. She was clinging to the precipice above a pit of madness—if she swallowed just one more drop, she knew she would slip over the edge; her mind finally unhinged.

As the burning venom filled her mouth, Penelope felt as though she was drowning in fire. She tried to move, but her numbed limbs still hung heavy by her sides. If she could just twist her head to one side...

Penelope strained to move her neck, willing the frozen muscles into life. As they spasmed in reply, she twisted herself sideways, retching as the acrid liquid spilled from her lips. The taste of it sent a fresh wave of nausea shuddering through her body, the venom-soaked bile pooling on the stone floor beside her until there was nothing left to bring up.

Gasping for air, Penelope lay there in the darkness for what felt like an age. A skull-splitting headache thumped in her brain, but the scurrying spiders that had filled her mind were gone, the shadows of their webs slowly fading. Wincing, she slowly raised herself up on her elbows, her eyes straining against the gloom.

The cell door was locked, the shutters drawn across its small, barred window. There was no sign of Bradburn anywhere. With a sudden shiver of realization, Penelope knew where he would be. She remembered Lady Cambridge's command, the glass vials of spider venom clinking in her palm. *Administer a double dose to every patient.* She had to stop Bradburn before it was too late.

As Penelope scrabbled to her feet, she felt something metallic clatter against her hand in the half-light. Reaching down, her fingers closed around the copper handle of a bedpan. She could feel the rough edges of words carved into its surface; the madness that had possessed Fitzgerald had forced him to write even on this. Penelope tightened her grip, feeling the weight of it in her hand. Maybe she could use it to get her own message out.

Hurrying to the door, Penelope pulled her arm back and, with all the strength she could muster, hammered the bedpan against the bars of the cell. A metallic clang rang out—a deafening noise to wake the sane and the mad alike. Penelope pulled her arm back again, striking the copper pan against the bars until every muscle in her body ached.

Clang. Clang. Clang.

In reply, Penelope heard a thudding sound echo down the corridor; cell doors shaking as patients thumped their fists against the wood.

Bang. Bang. Bang.

The hammering sound resounding through the walls of the asylum matched the thumping inside her skull. Message received.

Penelope stepped back exhausted, the bedpan falling from her fingers with a clatter as her strength gave way. Then the door to the cell slammed open with a crash and Bradburn's hulking figure stood framed in the doorway.

He leapt toward her, his brutish face red with rage.

"You meddling little twixter!" Bradburn roared, grabbing Penelope by her neck and pulling her face close to his. "What have you done?"

Penelope tried to pull herself free from his clutches, but she was too weak to fight back. She could feel his grimy fingers tightening around her neck.

"You've woken them all," he snarled, his sour breath scouring her skin. "The whole blasted lot of them. They're hammering fit to wake Morris himself. Make them stop."

Penelope could feel the blood pounding in her brain. As Bradburn squeezed the air from her lungs, she had just enough breath to croak a single word in reply.

"No."

With a howl of frustration, Bradburn tightened his fingers around her throat, squeezing with every ounce of his strength.

"Well, you'll sleep for good then," he snarled.

As his throttling grip narrowed, Penelope saw a darkness crowding in on all sides again. She felt herself begin to fall backward into an immense black web, but she knew that this time there would be no return. From what seemed like a great distance, she heard the sound of Monty's voice—*Stop him!*—and then Bradburn's hands were torn from her throat.

Gasping for breath, Penelope swooned, falling toward the hard stone floor, but before she could hit, firm hands reached out to cushion her fall. She felt herself lowered gently down until she was sat slumped against the wall of the cell. Through blinking eyes, she saw Alfie crouching by her side, his face pale with worry. On the other side of the cell, Monty and Dr. Morris were struggling to hold back Bradburn's brawny arms as a stream of orderlies piled into the cell to subdue him.

"Penny, are you all right?" Alfie asked her, his eyes shining with concern.

As her breath came in sharp juddering gasps, Penelope slowly nodded her head.

"I'm fine," she replied in a shredded whisper. She rubbed her neck, feeling the bruise of Bradburn's fingers against the skin there. "It's over now."

XVIII

"Mystery writer solves Bedlam Mystery." Holding that week's edition of the *Illustrated London News* in front of him, Alfie cleared his throat as he prepared to read the rest of the newspaper story. At her desk in the *Penny Dreadful's* office, Penelope rested her chin on her cupped hands, gazing up at Alfie with a look of weary indulgence as she prepared to hear the report yet again.

"A sinister criminal plot has recently been uncovered at the Bethlem Royal Hospital," Alfie continued, reading aloud from the paper. "In the weeks leading up to Christmas, patients at the hospital, one of London's leading asylums for the treatment of the mentally deranged, found themselves in the grip of a baffling condition. Every night, the residents of the asylum awoke with the uncontrollable urge to write, filling countless pages of text with outlandish visions.

After exhausting all fields of medical inquiry, doctors at the hospital called on the assistance of Mr. Montgomery Flinch, the bestselling author and editor of the acclaimed literary magazine, the *Penny Dreadful*. Using his knowledge of the uncanny, Mr. Flinch investigated the mysterious events and made a momentous discovery. A hospital orderly named Joseph Bradburn, aged thirty-four, had for some months been administering to the patients a poison that caused these delusions. Only through Mr. Flinch's swift actions was Bradburn caught in the act of poisoning and finally apprehended. Although the motives for this despicable crime as yet remain undiscovered, speaking to this newspaper, the author assured his legions of readers that the full story of this remarkable mystery would be told in his next tale of terror."

"And indeed it will!" The door to the office was flung open and Monty's voice boomed across the room. Shaking wintry squalls of sleet from his shoulders, Monty stepped inside, closing the door behind him with a slam. The actor's already flushed face was illuminated by a broad grin and, under his arm, he carried a stack of newspapers. He spilled them out on the desk in front of Penelope, and she saw Monty's triumphant face peering out from their front pages beneath a welter of headlines.

AUTHOR CAPTURES BEDLAM POISONER
BESTSELLING WRITER BRINGS
MYSTERY TO A CLOSE

MONTGOMERY FLINCH DOESN'T FLINCH IN
THE FACE OF DANGER

"I'm the talk of the town," cried Monty. "I can barely leave the door of my club without being mobbed. On my way here, I was stopped countless times by readers eager to learn the truth behind this Bedlam mystery."

Draping his overcoat on the stand, he sank down on the chair in front of Penelope's desk. Meeting her gaze, Monty greeted Penelope with a charming smile.

"And how is the story coming along, my dear?"

Underneath her furrowing brow, Penelope's eyes flashed at Monty's impudence. After all she had gone through to unravel the mystery, this was what she was left with: Monty's puffed-up face staring out from the front page of every newspaper. Their headlines acclaimed him as a hero, while she was stuck in here trying to write the first installment of Montgomery Flinch's latest tale.

As Penelope opened her mouth to remind Monty of his place, her thoughts flicked back to that terrible night at Bedlam: Bradburn's hands tightening around her throat, his fingers squeezing the life from her veins. If Monty and Alfie hadn't burst through the door of the cell when they had… Her irritation faded as quickly as it had come.

"The story is coming along well," she told Monty, quickly shuffling the papers on her desk to hide the blank sheet that lay in front of her. She glanced up at Alfie as he began to read yet another story aloud.

"And listen to this—"

Penelope cut him off with a brisk shake of her head. "Do we have to hear any more reports of Montgomery Flinch's heroics?" she asked in a pleading tone. "I'm sure Monty is getting quite tired of hearing the same tale all the time."

"Nonsense," Monty replied with relish. "Let the boy speak."

"It's not about Monty this time." Alfie thrust the newspaper toward Penelope and then pointed to a brief report at the bottom of the page. "This is about Lady Cambridge."

"Let me see," said Penelope. Taking hold of the newspaper, she began to read, a frown returning to her face as she did so.

FATAL FIRE IN LONDON

A grand street in South Kensington was the scene late on Monday night of a disastrous fire, which resulted in the death of at least seven people. The scene of this calamity was Stanley House in South Kensington, the London residence of Lady Cambridge, the wife of the late Lord Cambridge. The fire broke out while a dense fog was prevailing, and originated in the basement of the property. The alarm was first raised in the early hours of Tuesday morning by a neighbor who saw flames and smoke pouring out of the windows. Firemen were called, but by the time of their arrival, the fire had so far advanced that the house was almost entirely burnt out. In the cold light of day, a total of seven bodies were recovered from the smoking ruins and Lady Cambridge is believed to be among the dead.

Penelope flung the newspaper across her desk in annoyance. That night in Bedlam when the police had finally arrived to cart Bradburn off in handcuffs, she'd told them all about Lady Cambridge and how her guiding hand was behind the sinister plot. The thin-faced inspector had listened impatiently as she poured out the whole story, but then shook his head in amused disbelief. Patting her on the head, he'd called for Dr. Morris to prescribe her something for the hysteria which had obviously been brought on by the shock of her ordeal.

It was only days later that Bradburn, with the threat of the gallows hanging over his head, had started squealing like a stuck pig. His confession confirmed the truth of Penelope's claims, but by then it was too late. Stanley House lay in ruins, the filing cabinets in its hidden basement room burned to cinders. Lady Cambridge's scheme to harvest the spiders' secrets before the new century dawned had perished with her, the Midnight Papers all turned to ash and scattered by the wind.

Seeing the disappointed expression on Penelope's face, Alfie tried to comfort her.

"Don't brood about what happened," he said. "At least Lady Cambridge can't do anymore harm now. And think about what a story it will make. Change a few names here and there and you've got yourself the next bestselling issue of the *Penny Dreadful*—a true-life tale of terror to keep the readers rushing to the bookstands."

"Speaking of the next issue of the *Penny Dreadful*." From his desk at the back of the office, Wigram slowly rose to his feet, a thick wedge of envelopes held in his hand. "If we've all finished musing on past adventures, there is plenty of work to do in the here and now. The January edition of the magazine is due to go to press on New Year's Eve—that's three days' time. If you want to have a magazine fit to publish when the new century dawns, I'd suggest you get to work on answering the letters to the editor."

The elderly lawyer placed the bundle of letters at the top of the in-tray at the corner of Penelope's desk. Glancing across, her heart sank at the sight of the mountain of mail waiting there. Penelope looked up into her guardian's eyes, her fair-skinned face drawn in its most beguiling expression.

"Would you not be able to edit the letters page for this issue?" she asked. "It's just that with the lead story still to write..."

Wigram's stern countenance was unmoved by Penelope's gentle persuasion. The craggy lines creasing his brow deepened as he shook his head firmly.

"And I have got printer's invoices to pay, advertisements to place, and deliveries to arrange," he replied. "I've spent quite enough time covering your duties while you have been off gallivanting around Bedlam."

His gaze swiveled toward Monty, who was sat staring admiringly at his own photograph on the front page of the *Pall Mall Gazette*. Inside, the paper's interview with the author ran across three pages, although the nosy journalist Barrett's byline was conspicuous by its absence. The *Gazette's* editor had agreed to Penelope's request that Mr. Barrett should be taken off the Montgomery Flinch story for good in return for their exclusive interview.

"Perhaps Mr. Maples could help you to whittle down the letters we've received from Montgomery Flinch's most ardent admirers," Wigram suggested. "I imagine he wouldn't find that too taxing a task."

At the mention of his name, Monty glanced up, the satisfied smile on his face quickly fading as he met the lawyer's stern stare. Straightening in his chair, he promptly nodded his agreement.

"I'd be delighted to help in any way that I can."

"Good," Wigram replied curtly. "I'll leave you both to get on with it."

With a sigh, Penelope pushed the papers on her desk to one side and reached for the topmost letter. She sliced open the envelope then handed the paper knife to Monty as he leaned over the in-tray to retrieve the next. Penelope quickly glanced through the contents of the letter, an appeal from the manufacturer of a patented ball-point pen for Montgomery Flinch to endorse their product. Crumpling the paper into a ball, Penelope dropped the letter into the wastebasket beside her desk.

Gradually, the pile of letters began to diminish, the two of them each taking it in turn to slice open an envelope and read the letter inside. Requests for signed photographs of Montgomery Flinch, missives scrawled in bright green ink criticizing his plot twists, pleas for assistance from budding authors desperate for help with their own stories. Fretfully, Penelope brushed her long hair back from her face. At this rate, she was never going to find any letters that were fit to print in the pages of the *Penny Dreadful*.

Reaching for the next letter, she carefully slid the paper knife under the seal. Tipping the envelope, a stiff printed card dropped out onto the desk in front of her.

The Society of Illustrated Periodicals and Literary Magazines

Burlington House, Piccadilly, London

To the proprietor and editor of the *Penny Dreadful*,

You are cordially invited to attend an extraordinary meeting of the Society of Illustrated Periodicals and Literary Magazines. This event for the proprietors, editors, and contributors to London's finest journals is to announce a prestigious new literary competition which will be open to all attending. The winning entrant to the competition will receive a prize of £20,000.

Further details will be revealed at the meeting which will be held on the evening of Friday the 29th of December at seven o'clock sharp, Burlington House, Piccadilly. Drinks will be served at six thirty.

Please RSVP by return telegram.

Penelope's eyes glittered at the thought of the prize. Twenty thousand pounds—an unimaginable sum. It must be a typographical error. Surely the prize could only be £200, maybe £2,000 at most. There was only one way to find out. Turning the invitation over in her hands, she glanced up at the calendar on the wall. Today was Thursday, the twenty-eighth of December.

She called out across the office to Alfie who was standing at Wigram's desk, the two of them inspecting a ledger of printers' invoices.

"Alfie—I want you to send a telegram for me." As Alfie nodded in acknowledgment of her request, Penelope turned back toward Monty. "And Monty, you're going to need to get your dinner jacket cleaned."

Monty glanced up from his task, halfway through scrawling his signature across a picture of himself which he had clipped from one of the morning papers.

"Why?" he asked. "What's the occasion?"

"Montgomery Flinch needs to make an appearance among the cream of literary society," Penelope replied. "There's a competition to be won."

XIX

Long before six thirty there was a line of carriages stretching down Piccadilly, each awaiting its turn at the entrance in the shadow of the grand mansion house. Beneath its high arched windows, an array of footmen in black and gold livery ushered guests in evening dress from their vehicles and through the vaulted stone archway. As the late December mists swirled around their tailcoats, the guests hurried through an ornate set of double doors and into the brightness of Burlington House.

Penelope, Monty, and Wigram loitered inside the entrance hallway. Both Wigram and Monty stood stiff-necked in their winged collars and white bow ties, while Penelope wore a cerise evening gown, its bustle trailing her skirt behind her. The lobby was crowded with guests, sombre middle-aged men with muttonchop whiskers and bushy moustaches, dandyish young men in colorful silk waistcoats, and lean, pale-faced gentlemen hanging with a melancholy air at the fringes of the crowd. Scores of waiters carrying trays of drinks and canapés weaved their way through the throng. Penelope was the only girl there; in fact, she was the only member of the fairer sex to be seen.

"I do wish you hadn't come here tonight," Wigram muttered, standing close to Penelope as they surveyed the gathering in front of them. "We don't want to draw any unnecessary attention to your role at the *Penny Dreadful*. I could have chaperoned Mr. Maples perfectly well on my own."

Behind them, Monty lifted a handful of canapés from the tray of a passing waiter and stuffed them in his mouth. He dusted the crumbs from his hands before quickly taking another vol-au-vent.

"This is my kind of party," he said with a wolfish grin.

Penelope shook her head. Looking around the room, she saw H. G. Wells, H. Rider Haggard, Rudyard Kipling, and Arthur Conan Doyle, as well as countless more authors whose faces she had only previously seen peering out from pages of book reviews. The lobby of Burlington House was filled with the great and the good of literary London; everyone drawn here by the promise of the prize.

"This is where I should be," she told her guardian firmly. "I write the stories—the *Penny Dreadful* is my magazine. It's only right that I get a chance to taste a little of Montgomery Flinch's fame.

Besides, I want to hear more about this prize. It can't possibly be twenty thousand pounds—you could buy Burlington House itself with that kind of money. Something's not quite right here and I want to find out what it is."

From out of the throng, a rakish-looking gentleman dressed in a brightly striped waistcoat sprang toward Monty. Beneath a drooping handlebar moustache, a wide grin split the man's face as he took hold of Monty's hand and pumped it vigorously.

"Monty!" he cried, clapping the bewildered actor on the shoulder. "As I live and breathe it's you."

Monty's face quickly paled, a flicker of panic visible behind his eyes as he tried to extricate his hand from the man's grasp.

"Er, so good to see you," he managed to stutter in reply.

Penelope turned on her heels to face the dapper gentleman, fearful that Monty's cover had been blown.

"I read all about your Bedlam exploits in the papers at my club," the moustachioed man continued. "What a story that will make. Some of us only get to write our tales of mystery, but you seem to be living them, my dear fellow! How long is it since I last saw you? Was it at the Lodge?"

"Er, it could have been," ventured Monty.

Penelope saw the sweat beading Monty's forehead—he didn't have any idea who this was. She coughed once politely, anxious to turn the man's attention away from Monty to give him the chance to collect himself.

The man glanced across at her. "And who's this, Monty?" he asked, raising his eyebrow. "She's a little young to be your secretary, isn't she?"

Penelope shook her head, taken aback by the man's presumption. "I'm Mr. Flinch's niece, Miss Penelope Tredwell," she said, offering her hand in greeting. However, instead of the expected handshake, she felt the gentleman slip his business card into her hand by way of reply. She peered down at it in surprise.

Mr. Max Pemberton
Acclaimed Author, Intrepid Journalist, and Esteemed
Editor of *Cassell's Magazine*
c/o The Savage Club, 6–7 Adelphi Terrace,
Westminster, London

"We must talk about you coming to write for *Cassell's*," said Pemberton, turning the full glare of his attention back toward Monty. "I was only saying to Conrad just the other day that we ought to get some of Montgomery Flinch's fiction into the magazine. You've been wasting yourself on the pages of the *Penny Dreadful* for too long."

Penelope fumed as she listened to this brazen

attempt to poach her own stories. She coughed again, more pointedly this time. "My uncle has an exclusive agreement with the *Penny Dreadful.*"

Pemberton shook his head dismissively. "I haven't seen an agreement yet that my lawyers couldn't find a way around," he told Monty conspiratorially, curling his moustache as he spoke. "Anyway, I don't really see what business it is of yours." He fixed Penelope with a withering stare. "I'm sure your uncle will still be able to keep you in pretty dresses with the rates we pay at *Cassell's.*"

Catching sight of someone across the room, Pemberton raised his hand in greeting. "Arthur!" he called out as he plunged back into the crowd.

"Remember what I said," he called back to Monty over his shoulder. "Pop into the club and we can talk terms then."

"Who *was* that?" said Monty, shaking his head in confusion.

"The competition," Penelope replied, tearing Pemberton's card in two and depositing the pieces on a passing waiter's tray.

From out of the corner of her eye, she caught a glimpse of an unexpected face: the thin, boyish features of Mr. Robert Barrett, the journalist at the *Pall Mall Gazette*. He was munching on a canapé and the moment his gaze met hers, he swiftly looked away. Penelope narrowed her eyes. This wasn't part of the agreement. She turned toward Monty.

"Don't talk to anyone," she told him, "I'll be back in just one moment."

Swinging the bustle of her dress behind her, Penelope strode toward Barrett before Monty had the chance to argue. The journalist made a guilty start at her approach, his eyes flicking around the room as if in search of the exit.

"I didn't expect to see you here, Mr. Barrett," Penelope smiled disarmingly. "I thought that Mr. Flinch had made it quite clear to your editor what his side of the bargain was. The *Pall Mall Gazette's* exclusive interview with Montgomery Flinch was only granted on the condition that your harassment of him ceased."

Barrett scowled. "Don't worry, I'm just going," he snapped in reply. "I wouldn't want to upset Mr. Flinch, would I? My editor's already put me right on that score. He said that he will stick me behind a desk reviewing bad poetry and books for children for the rest of my career if I go within a mile of Montgomery Flinch."

Glancing across the room, Barrett fixed Monty with a grudgeful glare. "Your uncle can keep his secrets—whatever they are. I'm not interested anymore."

His eyes flicked back to Penelope, a forced smile fixed to his lips. "I shall bid you good night, Miss Tredwell. Please pass on my regards to Mr. Flinch—I'm sure he'll understand why I don't say farewell in person."

With that, Barrett turned on his heel. Penelope watched as he weaved his way through the throng of authors and out through the grand double doors into the darkness outside. Finally satisfied that he was gone, she slowly walked back toward Monty and Mr. Wigram. As she rejoined them, her guardian frowned.

"Speaking to the press again I see," he said with a disapproving tone. "You need to be careful, Penelope, that you don't end up becoming the story."

Penelope shook her head with a smile. "The only story that Mr. Barrett will be writing for the *Gazette* is a review of *Kidnapped by Cannibals* or some other boy's own adventure. He's not going to give Montgomery Flinch any more trouble."

Before she could explain herself further, the sound of a bell rang out. High on the wall, in an alcove above the lobby, a grand clock chimed seven times.

As if in answer, the doors to the meeting room swung open and an elderly, distinguished-looking gentleman stood framed in the entrance. He clapped his hands twice to call for attention and gradually the hubbub of noisy conversation faded into silence.

"The extraordinary meeting of the Society of Illustrated Periodicals and Literary Magazines is now called to order," he announced. "If you could just make your way through to the meeting room, gentlemen, then we can get things under way."

A ripple of excitement spread through the lobby, and then Penelope, Monty, and Wigram followed the lines of authors as they eagerly filed into the meeting room. Through the crowd of bobbing heads, Penelope could see a raised dais at the front of the room. In the center of the platform, a lectern stood empty while the authors settled themselves on long oak benches facing the stage. However, when Penelope reached the door, a long arm stretched out in front of her, blocking the entrance.

"I'm sorry, Miss."

She looked up to see the tall, gray-whiskered gentleman who had called the meeting to order barring her path.

"This meeting is for authors, editors, and proprietors only. No children allowed."

Penelope felt a resentful wave of anger welling up inside, although she kept this well hidden. The *Penny Dreadful* was her magazine—she was its editor, lead author, and publisher. Montgomery Flinch wouldn't exist without the stories she wrote.

"I am an author," she replied with a simpering smile. If she couldn't sneak into the meeting, perhaps a little coquettish charm would do the trick.

"Now, Penelope, I'm sure this gentleman is far too busy to listen to your foolish fancies." Penelope felt her guardian's hand rest on her shoulder.

"Writing for your school magazine doesn't make you the next Jane Austen, you know."

She glanced up at her guardian. As she met his gaze, Wigram's hooded eyes flashed in warning.

"I think it would be best if you just wait here," he said pointedly, "while Mr. Flinch and I hear more about this prestigious new literary prize. I'm sure you will be able to find a quiet spot to indulge in some embroidery."

Behind them, the last few authors still waiting to enter the meeting room were starting to grumble. Penelope slowly nodded her head. Her guardian's words infuriated her, but she knew why he had said them. There was no way she could get into that meeting room now without making a scene.

"Fine," she replied, tossing her hair back with a shrug, "I'll wait in the lobby."

As a relieved smile crept across his face, Wigram nodded graciously. Then, with a ruddy-cheeked Monty by his side, they led the last of the authors into the meeting room before the doors closed behind them with a slam.

Penelope stood there for a moment, silently fuming as she stared at the closed doors. She could write half of the hacks in there under the table. Yet she was stuck out here while the greatest literary prize London had ever seen was unveiled inside. A sudden clattering sound pulled Penelope's attention away from the fug of indignant thoughts swirling around her mind.

Glancing to her left, she saw a line of waiters trooping through a second set of doors. Their trays were loaded with half-finished glasses and, as the doors swung open in front of them, Penelope could hear the chatter of voices from the meeting room grow louder. Maybe there was another way in.

Penelope slipped through the doors before they swung shut again. Ahead of her, the waiters were traipsing along a dimly lit corridor. The babble of conversation was even louder now. Halfway along the corridor on the right, Penelope saw a small galleried window looking out over the meeting room, screened by a pair of thick velvet curtains.

Hurrying down the corridor, Penelope hid herself in the folds of the curtain, her cerise dress almost invisible against the red velvet. From her vantage point, she could see the whole of the meeting room laid out in front of her. Four domed chandeliers hung from its vaulted ceiling, shining with the steady brilliance of electric light, while from the walls, a legion of white-bearded gentlemen stared down from their portraits on to the proceedings below. The room was packed to bursting, rows of writers, editors, and publishers squeezed uncomfortably on to the hard oak benches facing the stage.

Penelope glimpsed Monty sitting in the front row, sandwiched between Arthur Conan Doyle and H. Rider Haggard, while her guardian, Mr.

Wigram, was standing at the far side of the room. His arms were folded across his chest as he stood deep in conversation with the editor of *Cassell's Magazine*, a frown spreading across his features as Pemberton's gestures became ever more animated.

Meanwhile, at the front of the room, the tall, gray-whiskered gentleman had climbed up onto the raised dais. He solemnly stepped forward to the front of the stage and, looking out over his gold-rimmed spectacles, rapped his knuckles against the lectern.

"Gentleman, if we are all quite ready to begin."

XX

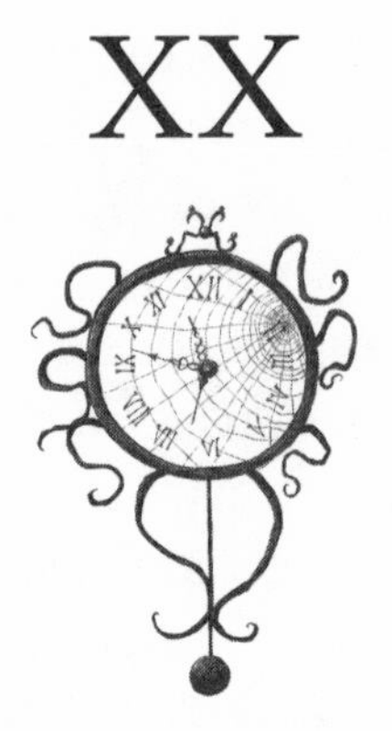

“As president of the Society of Illustrated Periodicals and Literary Magazines, I am pleased to see such an array of distinguished guests gathered here this evening.” Gripping the sides of the lectern, the gray-whiskered gentleman peered out at his audience, who were now listening with a respectful silence. “Before me are the finest voices in English literature and I have brought you together, gentlemen, to hear news of a dazzling new literary prize.”

Across the meeting room, there came the sound of creaking benches as the assembled authors leaned forward in their seats.

“In the past week,” the president continued, “the Society has been approached by an anonymous benefactor, who, in these last days of the nineteenth century, has proposed a thrilling literary challenge, a unique competition that comes with a breathtaking reward.”

His solemn features flushed as though he could barely contain his own excitement at the news he was sharing, and his hands cut the air in flurries of motion as he spoke.

"As we stand on the brink of the twentieth century, the challenge I lay down before you this evening, gentlemen, is for you to write and publish a story about the wonders of the new century that is to come. The author and magazine who are judged to have produced the winning story will share a prize of twenty thousand pounds."

A gasp rippled through the room, nobody having dared to believe until that moment that the size of the prize was true. Apart from a few of the literary giants seated in the front row, most of the authors gathered in the room were more used to scratching a living, selling their stories for tens of shillings not thousands of pounds. It was an incredible sum of money.

From her hiding place, Penelope's nerves started to jangle. The competition, the prize—it was all too good to be true. Something wasn't right here.

"What's the catch?"

The call from the floor of the meeting room echoed Penelope's own thoughts.

"The Society will publicize the competition," the president replied. "We have taken out advertisements which will be printed in all the daily newspapers tomorrow to inform the reading public of this exciting literary challenge. However, the competition itself has only one important rule—the winning story must be written and published before the new century dawns."

The room erupted in a chorus of protest, the authors' clamoring voices shouting out their concerns.

"But it's New Year's Eve in two days' time!"

"Impossible!"

"It can't be done."

"Gentlemen, gentlemen." The president raised his hands to calm the uproar. "If you don't think you can rise to the challenge then that's perfectly all right. However, think about the prize at hand if you do."

The room fell silent as his words hung in the air, all minds turning again to dreams of unimagined wealth. Then, from the back of the room, a portly man of about fifty rose to his feet, his face set in a suspicious expression.

"Who is going to judge this competition then?" he demanded. "I don't want to see another stitch-up like the Fraser Prize fiasco. Every single book on the shortlist was published by John Fraser himself!"

The president solemnly shook his head as knowing snickers of laughter rippled along the long oak benches.

"Our benefactor will judge the competition herself," he replied.

At this comment, Penelope's vague feelings of

unease began to sharpen into a sense of dread. The pieces of the jigsaw slotted into place at last: the challenge to write a story about the century to come, the impossible deadline, the astounding prize, and the mysterious lady who was behind it all. Her fingers whitening as she gripped the heavy velvet curtain more tightly around herself, Penelope knew who had brought them all here tonight.

Back in the meeting room, the doors to the side of the stage swung open. From the wings, a long line of waiters emerged, their brimming trays replenished with drinks again. Moving along the rows of oak benches, they presented each of the gentlemen sitting there with a tall glass of fizzing champagne. Monty snatched his glass from the tray with an enthusiastic hand as, from behind the lectern, the president began to speak again.

"And to celebrate the inauguration of this grand new prize, I propose a toast, gentlemen."

He waited until every single guest in the meeting room had a charged glass in their hand, and then as the waiters filed out of the room once more, the president brought his own glass aloft.

"Here's to the twentieth century and your stories that will bring it alive."

"Hear, hear!"

As one, the assembled audience stood and raised their glasses aloft before taking a swig of the sparkling liquid. From the galleried window,

Penelope watched on aghast as a strange silence suddenly fell across the room.

Every figure was standing motionless, the authors frozen in position with the now-empty glasses fixed to their lips. At the front of the stage, she could see the president of the Society, his pinched features now as gray as his whiskers. Behind his gold-rimmed glasses, his eyes were glazed and unfocused as though held in some kind of trance. Then the glass slipped from his fingers and crashed to the floor where it shattered into countless pieces.

As the sound of the splintering glass echoed through the silence, a dark figure stepped from the shadows at the side of the stage. It was a tall woman, dressed in a flowing black gown, her shoulders muffled in a black fur stole and her face shrouded by a thick black veil. Arriving at the front of the stage, she carefully stepped past the circle of shattered glass and then pulled back her veil to gaze out at the audience beneath her.

Penelope gasped.

A stray lock of dark hair fell across the fur stole, as from beneath the veil the strikingly beautiful features of Lady Cambridge were revealed. Her face was deadly pale, the hard red line of her lips set in a disconcerting smile while her blue eyes shone with an unnatural fire.

"So this is the cream of literary London?" she sneered coldly. "The finest imaginations of our generation snuffling like pigs in a trough in search of the prize. I knew that the promise of twenty thousand pounds would be enough to bring you all here tonight."

Lady Cambridge stared out at the rows of silent authors, still frozen, seemingly hypnotized by the cold beauty of her glare.

"However, I'm afraid that the rules of this competition have changed somewhat. The drinks with which you have just toasted your own success were laced with a special preparation of the venom of the dream-weaver spider." She glanced down at Monty's spellbound figure in the front row, icy daggers in her eyes. "The last of my supplies thanks to the meddling of that niece of yours. This will give you all the inspiration you need."

Monty stood perfectly motionless; his ruddy cheeks now pale as the glass in his hand trembled slightly. From her hiding place, shrouded in the heavy velvet curtains, a cold shiver crept down Penelope's spine, fearful that at any moment, Lady Cambridge could turn her gaze toward her.

"This special preparation is twenty times more potent than the venom I used to dose the patients at Bedlam. Their minds were already broken, but yours need to be bent to my will, so I've mixed the solution to complete saturation with the mesmerizing venom of the flat-sand scorpion. With the power of your words, I want you to hypnotize the entire city."

Her chilling gaze glittered with menace.

"The stories that will flow from your pens will not only chart the future to come," Lady Cambridge continued, her aristocratic voice cold and imperious, "but will send everyone who reads them spiraling into the same madness that possesses you now. Under my command, you will weave subliminal orders into the sentences you write, hypnotic triggers to take control of your readers' minds. These subliminal orders will bear the imprint of the dream-weaver spider; a parasitic code spreading its poison like a plague. Soon every reader of your penny dreadfuls and shilling shockers will be haunted by the same visions that stalked the cells at Bedlam. All across London, they will pick up their pens with twitching fingers and write for me the answers that I have been seeking. With the power of all these minds working together, I will be able to unlock the secrets of the next thousand years. The prophecy will be fulfilled. As the New Year dawns, your words will seal my destiny as the most powerful woman in history. Already, the agents of a dozen enemy powers petition me for the secrets I hold. The auction of the century will commence on January the first."

She brought her black gloved hands together with a thunder crack.

"Now get back to your Grub Street offices and filthy writers' garrets and set down for me the stories that will make my fortune."

Roused from their stupor, the audience turned as one and silently began to file out of the meeting room, shuffling their way past the long lines of benches and out into the lobby beyond. Penelope glimpsed Monty and Wigram in the midst of the crowd, their faces still frozen, emotionless, and their eyes oddly glazed. As the society's president slumped forward over the lectern, Lady Cambridge swept the train of her black gown behind her as she disappeared back into the shadows at the side of the stage.

Penelope was torn, her mind still spinning at what she had heard. Should she follow Lady Cambridge or try and break this spell that she had cast over Monty, Mr. Wigram, and the rest of literary London? She shivered. Lady Cambridge had come back from the dead once already. She needed help before she faced her again.

Darting back behind the curtains, she hurried down the dimly lit corridor. Pushing her way through the doors, Penelope stepped out into the crowded lobby. A mob of top hats and evening suits barred her path; the entranced authors, editors, and publishers milling silently as they waited to leave Burlington House.

"Wake up!" she cried out as she pushed her way through the throng. With sharp elbows, she battled her way forward, the glazed faces of the men she pushed past glancing down at her with deadened eyes, as though she was an apparition out of a dream. Nobody tried to stop her; they just carried on walking toward the exit like sleepers in the night. Penelope caught a glimpse of Monty and Wigram ahead of her, the two men departing through the ornate double doors into the darkened street outside.

In desperation, Penelope launched herself forward, squeezing her way through the crowd. She felt the heel of her boot jab into a foot, and glancing back in apology saw Arthur Conan Doyle's face crumpled in pain. The press of people around her was reaching a bottleneck as the entrance lay only a few feet away. With one last shove, Penelope barged her way past them and out through the doors.

The cold night air hit her like a slap across the face; thick fingers of mist swirling across the courtyard of Burlington House. Squinting into the gloom, Penelope tried to determine which way Monty and Wigram had gone. Through the archway to her right, she could see a line of hansom cabs, the light from their lanterns straining against the night. At the steps of the nearest cab, she saw two familiar silhouettes, one tall and lean, the second rather broader in beam, climbing up into the carriage.

"Monty! Mr. Wigram!"

Penelope raced toward the cab, her heels clattering across the misty cobbles. As she reached the footplate, a shadowy face appeared at the cab's window; the thin, pinched features of her guardian dimly lit by a streetlamp.

"What do you want?"

Her guardian's bark echoed out into the night, wreaths of smoke clinging to his lips as he stared down at her with unblinking eyes.

"After Lady Cambridge appeared, I didn't know what to do." Penelope spoke quickly, the words tumbling over one another in her confusion. "When you all drank the champagne, I thought you had been—"

"We don't have time to listen to the girl's nonsense." Monty's voice boomed out from the interior of the cab. "My mind is crawling with stories—I need to feel a pen between my fingers."

With a distracted expression on his face, Wigram half-turned and nodded his agreement.

"Yes, of course," he sighed. His voice was distant, as though he was listening to the scratching inside his own mind. "The stories must be written."

He turned back to face Penelope, his stern features wreathed in shadows.

"Go home, young lady," he told her. "Mr. Flinch and I have a magazine to publish."

Penelope watched horrified as, with a gesture toward the driver, her guardian briskly turned away from the window. As the driver whipped the horses, the hansom cab rattled across the cobbles and disappeared down Piccadilly, the thick fog soon swallowing even the sound of the horses' hooves. Standing alone in the darkness, she felt lost, trapped in a huge web spun by Lady Cambridge's cunning. The nightmare wasn't over—it was only just beginning.

XXI

"So they just left you standing there in the middle of Piccadilly?"

Alfie shook his head in disbelief as he trotted by Penelope's side, the two of them turning left off the Strand as they headed for the *Penny Dreadful's* office. An early morning mist was still clinging to the streets as they dodged past the empty barrows pushed by costermongers and street traders on their way back from Covent Garden Market. At a newsstand on the corner, a billboard proclaimed:

NEW LITERARY PRIZE GRIPS LONDON

Penelope nodded. Her own face was as grim as the gray December dawn.

"It was like they were in some kind of trance. I don't think they even knew who I was. Mr. Wigram didn't return home at all last night, and there's been no sign of Monty at his club. They must have come here."

They were nearing the broad stone steps that led up to the office.

"And you think Lady Cambridge is behind all this?"

"I saw her, Alfie," Penelope replied. "Lady Cambridge is still alive. She must have started that fire just to cover her tracks, burning down her own home and disappearing into the night with the prophecies of the century to come in her possession. And now she plans to write the final chapter." Penelope shivered as she recalled the icy gaze of the black-veiled widow staring out from the stage. "She drugged them all—the minds of the finest writers in London bent to her will. And if her plan works, she'll soon have the whole of the city under her spell."

Alfie's face paled as he started to climb the steps, but when he reached the top, he threw his shoulders back in a resolute stance.

"Maybe it's worn off by now," he said confidently as his hand grasped the door handle.

Penelope hung back, suddenly frightened at what they would find. Since her parents had died, Mr. Wigram had been like a father to her—a strict and unsmiling guardian for the most time, but someone who cared for her nonetheless. If he didn't recognize her again...

"It's locked." Alfie turned back to Penelope, the

handle rattling uselessly beneath his fingers. "But there's someone in there—I can see them."

Shaking off her nagging sense of fear, Penelope stepped forward and peered through the frosted glass at the top of the door. She could see the soft glow of the gas lamps lighting the office. Beneath these, two shadowy silhouettes sat hunched behind facing desks, the faint clicking of typewriter keys the only sound that could be heard through the glass.

"Mr. Wigram!" Alfie rapped on the door knocker, its sudden thump causing Penelope to jump in surprise. She turned toward Alfie with a hiss.

"Don't!"

Alfie froze with his hand in midair, the door knocker dangling from his fingers. Mouthing an apology, he gently laid the knocker to rest. From behind the door, the noise of clattering keys came to a halt. Then there was the shrill shriek of a chair being pushed backward followed by the sound of footsteps approaching.

"Someone's coming."

The heavy door slowly swung back to reveal Wigram's haggard features peering around the frame.

"What do you want?" he asked in a low growl.

Penelope took a nervous step backward, shocked by her guardian's sharp tone and his shabby appearance. He was wearing the same rumpled evening suit as he had been the previous evening, its starched collars now wilting and the white bow tie hanging unfastened around his neck.

"We were worried, Mr. Wigram," Alfie replied, swallowing hard as the lawyer turned his venomous gaze on him. "Penny said you didn't come home last night and with everything that—"

"Too busy, too busy," Wigram hissed, snapping Alfie into silence. His fingers twitched and twisted, weaving invisible webs in the air. Deep in the gloom of the office behind him, Monty was hunched in front of a typewriter, his shadowy fingers pecking at the keys like nervous crows. The actor didn't even acknowledge their presence as he sat lost among the dreams that dripped from his fingers.

Penelope took a step forward to enter the office, but Wigram quickly pulled the door toward him, blocking her path. "Where do you think you're going?"

Her guardian's frown tightened, his face creasing like an angry troll's. His eyes were still set in the same unblinking glare that seemed to peer straight through Penelope without seeing her at all.

"To work," Penelope replied, her voice shaking. "The *Penny Dreadful* is my magazine, remember?"

Wigram shook his head with a scowl.

"The *Penny Dreadful* belongs to Montgomery Flinch," he hissed in reply. "Now leave us alone."

The door slammed shut in Penelope's face.

Despairing, she turned toward Alfie, who looked back at her with a bewildered expression.

"This isn't right," he muttered. "There's got to be some way of getting through to him." Alfie grabbed the knocker and started hammering it against the door with a heavy fist. "Mr. Wigram! Monty! Please let us in!"

He paused, waiting for an answer. But the only reply that came was the sound of several bolts being slid across the door.

With a sinking heart, Penelope shook her head.

"It's no use," she told Alfie as he lifted the door knocker again. "They're in her power. Lady Cambridge is running the *Penny Dreadful* now."

Alfie let the knocker fall back into place with a hopeless clunk.

"What can we do then?"

"I don't know," Penelope replied, shaking her head as she stared at the locked door, the name of the *Penny Dreadful* etched across the frosted glass. This was her magazine—Montgomery Flinch was her creation. A cold, creeping fury rose up inside her, Penelope's fingers whitening as they slowly clenched into fists. She wouldn't let Lady Cambridge take this away. She was going to find a way to stop her.

"Come on," she said to Alfie, turning away from the door and heading down the steps to the street below. "Let's go."

A confused expression clung to Alfie's face as he scrambled to keep up with Penelope's brisk stride.

"But where are we going?" he asked.

"Most of the authors in London were at that meeting last night," Penelope replied, her face set in a determined frown. "We're going to find out if they're under Lady Cambridge's spell as well."

"I'm so sorry, sir, but these two young imps just barged right past me."

Framed in the doorway, the butler bent his head in apology as Penelope and Alfie stood defiantly in front of him, just inside the threshold to the study. Through a long sash window, thin streaks of sunlight fell across the mahogany writing desk which sat beneath it, its surface crowded with manuscripts and papers. Turning in his chair, the hunched figure of a middle-aged man looked up questioningly at the interruption, the pen in his hand still racing across the page with scarcely a pause for thought. The plump walrus moustache perched on his top lip made him instantly recognizable to anyone who read his bestselling stories of scientific romance—*The Time Machine*, *The War of the Worlds,* and *The Invisible Man*—but the author's eyes were distant and glazed. He muttered under his breath as he turned back to his desk, scribbling frantically across the sheets of paper strewn there.

"I'll get them to leave right away," the butler reassured him.

"We're going nowhere," said Alfie, his arms folded tightly across his chest. "Not until we've spoken to Mr. Wells."

Oblivious to their presence, H. G. Wells sat bent over his desk, his pen continuously scratching across the page as he talked to himself in a low mumble. Penelope strained her ears to try to make out the words.

"Secrets of the flying machine...the land ironclad triumphant...a calculating machine the size of a thimble...the first men in the moon...the spiral of life...the end of the world."

"Now come along." The butler laid a firm hand on Penelope's shoulder, breaking her concentration. "I'm really going to have to insist that you both leave."

Penelope turned to face him, her eyes wide with concern.

"You know that something is wrong," she said. "Anyone can see that—so why won't you let me help him?"

The butler's mask of reserve cracked, and Penelope glimpsed for the first time the glimmer of doubt in his eyes.

"How long has he been like this?" she pressed.

The butler glanced nervously over Penelope's shoulder as though fearful of betraying his master's confidence, but Wells was still hunched over his writing desk, his pen scratching across the page without a pause.

"Since he returned home last night," the butler confided in a low voice. "He's not eaten, slept, or even changed his clothes—he has just sat there at his desk filling endless pages with his scribbles. I've never known him like this, even when he is writing one of his stories to a deadline for the monthly magazines."

Alfie glanced down as, from the edge of the desk, a loose sheaf of papers teetered and fluttered to the floor, but Wells carried on writing regardless.

"Can't you get him to stop?" he asked.

The butler shook his head firmly, a horrified expression fixed to his face. "I wouldn't dream of it. It's not my place."

Penelope stepped forward into the heart of the study, her slight figure dwarfed by the towering bookcases that lined the walls. "Well, I'll make it my place."

She reached out and rested her hand on the author's shoulder, trying to rouse him from his entranced state.

"Mr. Wells, Mr. Wells, can you hear me?"

Her voice was soft but insistent, yet Wells gave no sign that he heard it as the pen in his fingers scratched without a pause across the page. Penelope peered down at the words spilling from the pen.

Great cities teeming with millions of minds... the atom splits as the bombs rain down...a world overwhelmed by war...

Taking a deep breath, she gently caught hold of Wells's hand, trying to pluck the pen from his fingers.

"Mr. Wells," she pleaded. "You need to wake up."

His hand still grasping the pen, the author looked up at her. For a moment, beneath his bristling eyebrows, Wells's gray eyes swam into focus, seeing Penelope as though for the first time.

"Unhand me, child," he hissed. "My eyes have seen the glory—I have glimpsed the shape of things to come. Flickering visions of the future—they come so quickly—the triumphs and disasters, the inevitable and the unforeseen. There are the ideas for a thousand books swirling around my brain. I must get them down."

Snatching his hand away, Wells turned back to the page.

"You've been poisoned," Penelope told him, her sharp tone trying to break through the cloud of delirium that held the author in its grip. "These aren't your words—they're a dream of madness."

With an anguished howl, Wells turned again to face them. His eyes rolled upward, his features contorted with rage. With a barely suppressed anger, he slammed his fist against the desk.

"Get out! Get out!" he roared. "Kenton—get this creature out of here. They come to take my ideas—thieves and plagiarists all. Get her out!"

Almost apologetically, the butler's heavy hands came to rest on Penelope's shoulders. He steered her firmly toward the door as Alfie skulked out of the room in front of her. They could hear the sound of Wells raging behind them as they stepped into the corridor. The last thing Penelope saw before the study door closed was the author bent weeping over his writing desk, the pen in his hand still scratching across the page.

It was the same story everywhere else that they went. From Fleet Street to the Strand, from Bloomsbury to Pall Mall: all across London, on every door that they knocked, they found authors indisposed, magazine offices locked and bolted. But at every window, they could see shadowy shapes hunched over desks, the pens in their hands scratching endlessly across the page.

As the charcoal-gray sky finally faded to black and streetlamps flickered into life, Penelope and Alfie sat slumped on a bench in the shadow of the British Museum. The look of determination had slipped from Penelope's face and, as Alfie blew into his cupped hands to keep them warm, she shook her head in despair.

"It's hopeless. Lady Cambridge has the whole of literary London under her spell. There's no way of stopping her. When the magazines start to publish their stories, the whole of London itself will fall prey to this madness. What are we going to do?"

Alfie frowned.

"Maybe it won't work," he said, his wistful tone showing that he was clutching at straws. "Imagine Monty trying to write a story—he wouldn't know where to begin."

Penelope shuddered. She could imagine it only too well. The months she'd spent building Montgomery Flinch's reputation, the exquisitely crafted tales of terror that she'd written under his name—she could lose it all if Monty managed to put pen to paper.

The heavy clatter of horses' hooves and the sound of a wagon unloading pulled Penelope's thoughts away from this misery. At the news-stand on the corner, a young boy was carrying heaped bundles of papers from a delivery wagon. The news vendor, a tall, thin man, was crouched, stacking the newly delivered papers on his stand. As he finished, he turned and, with a bold hand, chalked a new headline across the newsstand board.

STOP PRESS—FIRST STORIES
OF A NEW CENTURY

Slipping the delivery boy a grubby handful of coins, the newsagent grabbed the topmost paper from his pile and bellowed:

"Special edition of the *Strand* magazine! Exclusive new story from the pen of Arthur Conan Doyle. Read all about his vision of the future!"

Penelope and Alfie stared at each other aghast. Beneath the glow of the streetlamp, the passing pedestrians started to crowd around the newsstand, eager to buy their copies of the magazine. Above their heads, thick trails of mist were spreading, ghostly fingers tightening their grip on the sky.

XXII

The dreams started that night. A huge spider web of black silken threads stretched across the city, capturing every reader in its snare. As copies of the *Strand* magazine sat on bedside tables, an army of sleepers slowly rose from their beds. With eyes glazed, their fingers scrabbled for something to write with, knocking lamps, books, and picture frames to the floor in their stupor. Frightened wives screamed as their sleeping husbands scratched strange messages into bedsteads, bewitched children filling their storybooks with frantic scribbles, deaf to their worried parents' pleas. Outside in the shivering frost, a tramp rolled over in the gutter, his grimy skin showing through the rips in his ragged clothes. Clutching torn pages of newsprint more tightly to his body for warmth, he reached out with a shaking hand. His fingers closed around a broken bottle lying next to him in the gutter and, raising it to the wall, he began to scratch a trembling message across the stone.

The World Is Gone Mad

And among this madness, an army of thieves were set loose across the city. Recruited by Lady Cambridge from the criminal underworld that lurked in London's shadows, these thieves had only one instruction: to steal the last installments of the Midnight Papers. In the dead of night, black-clad burglars broke in through fanlight windows; prowlers and picklocks creeping through the grand houses of Belgravia, Knightsbridge, Mayfair, and Sloane Square. As the dreamers sank back into a troubled sleep, her thieves gathered up their freshly inked papers, stealing out from the houses before the dull gray edges of dawn began to stain the sky and returning them to their mistress's lair.

The last day of the nineteenth century was here. New Year's Eve, 1899.

Penelope stood in front of the newsstand, reading the morning headlines as, next to her, Alfie leafed through the pages of that day's edition of the *Illustrated London News*.

CRIME WAVE HITS CITY—NIGHT ROBBERIES PLAGUE LONDON

REAL-LIFE MORIARTY BLAMED FOR STRING OF BURGLARIES

POLICE BAFFLED BY MYSTERIOUS BREAK-INS

Penelope's face furrowed in a frown as she tried to crack the riddle behind these headlines. Lady Cambridge's hand was somewhere behind all of this, she was sure of it. Behind her, the Thames curled lazily under the arches of Westminster Bridge as boats and barges, black with coal, crisscrossed the river. Beyond this, she glimpsed the Houses of Parliament, its gothic towers half-shrouded in mist. All along the embankment, a great tide of people hurried toward their places of work, no rest for them even on the eve of this new century.

"Penny."

Alfie tugged at her sleeve, pulling her gaze away from the rack of daily newspapers. He gestured to the side of the stand where the sour-faced vendor was unbundling a parcel of freshly printed papers, the printers' string still tied around them. The vendor cursed as the string snapped, spilling the papers across the pavement, and Penelope saw with a shudder the special editions of numerous magazines scattered among them. The *Graphic*, *Chambers's Journal*, the *Boy's Own Paper*, *Pearson's* magazine. On the front covers of each and every one, the headline *Visions of the Future* stood out in stark black letters, announcing the wondrous stories that could be found within. Mercifully, the *Penny Dreadful* wasn't among them.

Alfie stooped down to help the vendor retrieve the magazines, but as he picked up a copy of the *Boy's Own Paper* and started to leaf through its pages, Penelope snatched the magazine from his hand with a strangled cry.

"Don't!"

Startled, Alfie turned around, his eyes widening with surprise.

"I was only—"

Penelope dashed the magazine into the gutter, its front cover tearing as it landed.

"These stories are dangerous," she told him. Before she had a chance to explain herself further, the sound of a gruff bellow made Penelope suddenly flinch.

"Oi!"

She turned to see the beefy newspaperman advancing angrily toward her. In one hand, he had gathered up a loose sheaf of magazines, but his other hand was clenched into a fist.

"That's my blasted stock you're ruining, girl. Come here!"

For a split second, Penelope stood frozen. Then Alfie grabbed hold of her arm, dragging her to her senses as he shouted out a single word of warning.

"Run!"

Dodging past the street hawkers with their baskets arrayed on the pavement, Penelope and Alfie fled in the direction of Westminster Bridge. Quickly losing themselves in the torrent of people streaming down the street, Penelope glanced back through the crowd to see the red-faced vendor turn and aim a frustrated boot at a dog that was snuffling the discarded papers. She reached out for Alfie's arm, slowing him to a stroll.

"It's all right," she panted. "We've lost him."

Around them, the crowds hemmed in on all sides, sweeping them along like corks in a surging river. Silver-haired bankers, merchants, and lawyers, gray-suited clerks and porters, nurses wheeling tightly swaddled children for a morning stroll, the constant eddying tide of the London mob. The sky above looked like a great dome of slate, and half-melted snowflakes began to fall in a shower of sleet. Penelope pulled her scarf more closely around her neck as the sharp easterly wind filled her eyes with water.

"I wasn't going to read it, you know," Alfie muttered sullenly, pulling up the collar of his coat against the chill. "Although I don't see what harm it would've done if I had."

"Do you want to end up like Monty, H. G. Wells, and Mr. Wigram?" she snapped. "Driven half mad by the spiders in their minds? Just look around you—all of London is falling prey to their delusions!"

Alfie glanced up as they pushed their way through the buffeting crowd. He noticed for the first time the glazed look in the eyes of the people they passed. A bowler-hatted gentleman, with a copy of *Cassell's Magazine* tucked under his arm, was walking straight toward them. In his right hand he held a house brick pressed to his ear and was scowling as he jabbered wildly into the empty air. Alfie and Penelope had to quickly step to one side, pressing themselves against the wall as the man brushed past, still blindly ranting to nobody at all.

"He should be in the madhouse," Alfie whistled, shaking his head in disbelief.

Penelope stared out at the jostling crowds. Among the noisy bustle of cabs and carriages, most of the passers-by seemed to be half sleeping as they walked, their eyes heavy with tears, while others gazed awestruck at the empty skyline as though seeing wonders that weren't even there. Alfie followed her gaze, his forehead creasing in confusion.

"What can they all see?"

"The future," Penelope replied grimly. "The madness is spreading like a virus. We need to stop people from reading these stories—wake them up from this nightmare."

"How?" asked Alfie, his face flushed by the ice-cold wind.

Penelope looked down at the rolled-up newspaper

in Alfie's hand. Her eyes narrowed and the spark of an idea caught flame in her mind.

"We need to tell them what's really going on," she explained, her voice rising in excitement. "Get the newspapers to print the truth. Tell the world that Lady Cambridge is behind this outbreak of madness. Stop her before she changes the future forever."

Alfie shook his head, a doubtful expression on his face.

"Everybody thinks that Lady Cambridge is dead," he reminded her. "Nobody will believe us."

Penelope bristled at this suggestion.

"They've got to believe me," she replied indignantly. "Don't forget, I own the *Penny Dreadful*. I'm the bestselling author in Britain. I can make them listen to me. I will..."

Her voice trailed into silence as the realization slowly dawned. Whatever she said, nobody would pay her the slightest bit of attention. The whole world thought that Monty Maples was Montgomery Flinch. Her brilliant scheme to give the mysterious author a public face had been too successful. Penelope's face fell in disappointment and despair.

"You're right," she said. "There isn't a journalist in London who would listen to us now."

But even as she said these words, the face of a man swam to the front of her mind. She could see his lean, pockmarked features, the neatly trimmed moustache, and his suspicious eyes peering inquisitively back at her. A journalist who didn't believe that Montgomery Flinch was all that he claimed to be.

"That's it!"

Stepping out into the street, Penelope flung her hand out in front of her. A hansom cab was clattering at full pelt across the cobbles, and, thinking she had lost her mind, Alfie dashed into the street after her. With a horrified expression flashing across his face, the cabbie reined his horses to a halt, stopping only inches from where Penelope was standing.

The cabman leaned down from the driver's seat.

"What the blazes do you think you are doing?" he roared. "Get out of the road."

Shaking her head, Penelope clambered up into the cab, motioning for Alfie to climb in after her. As they settled in their seats, she turned to address the driver through the window at the top of the cab.

"Take us to Northumberland Street," she ordered him as the cab driver stared back at her, dumbfounded by her nerve. "The offices of the *Pall Mall Gazette*."

XXIII

"You've got to help us, Mr. Barrett," Penelope pleaded. "Time is running out."

She hurried down Fleet Street with Alfie by her side as the tall figure of the journalist strode a pace ahead of them, his overcoat buttoned against the cold. Above their heads, large black clouds were spreading out across the sky, thickening the darkness. As they passed beneath a streetlamp's pale moonlight glow, Penelope glanced nervously at her pocket watch. It was seven in the evening. Only five hours left until midnight and the end of the century. Lady Cambridge's prophecy was almost fulfilled.

Penelope and Alfie had spent most of the day trying to track the young journalist down. From the Northumberland Street offices of the *Pall Mall Gazette* to the pubs and taverns of Fleet Street, they had followed his trail, but the elusive correspondent had always been one step ahead of them. Only now as night drew in around them, had they finally spotted him, lurching from the doors of one pub and hurrying on to the next.

Penelope quickened her pace to keep up with Barrett as the tall journalist made a beeline toward the dimly lit windows of the tavern dead ahead. Above its door, a pub sign reading YE OLDE CHESHIRE CHEESE swung in the stiffening breeze.

The journalist shook his head, glancing down irritably at Penelope as she kept step by his side.

"I'm off duty," he told her bluntly. "Save it until next year and stop by the newspaper then."

"It'll be too late then," Penelope replied. "Look around you. There's a madness spreading across the city—the whole of London is losing its mind. Don't you want to know why?"

Barrett paused at the entrance to the pub, his hand on the door handle. The muffled noise from the drinkers inside seeped out as he turned to face them.

"It's New Year's Eve," he reminded her with a scornful smile. "The dawn of a new century. Everybody's going a little bit crazy. And, if you'll excuse me, I'll soon be joining them." As he pushed the door open, a tumult of voices, laughter, and clattering glasses spilled out into the street. "Good-bye, Miss Tredwell."

Her face hardening into a scowl, Penelope seethed at the man's ignorance. Here was the one person who could help them get the truth heard and he was about to disappear into a drunken haze. She had to do something.

"I'll give you the biggest story you've ever heard," she snapped. "A story that will make you the most famous journalist this country has ever seen."

Framed in the doorway, Barrett glanced back at her with a flicker of distrust. "Why should I believe you?"

Penelope looked him straight in the eye. Her long, dark hair fell across her pale face, but behind this her eyes were narrowed into a deadly serious stare.

"Because I'm Montgomery Flinch," she replied.

"It's the most ridiculous thing I've ever heard!"

Barrett pushed his pint glass away, beer slopping over its sides and spilling out across the cramped table as Penelope and Alfie sat there facing him. Around them in the dimly lit bar, the hubbub of conversation continued unabated. Grizzled newspapermen, their fingers stained with ink, sat along long wooden tables loaded with pots and glasses, the noise of their voices filling the room with raucous debate. The dark walls were ornamented with the framed front pages of Fleet Street's finest newspapers, each print representing a sensational scoop written by one of the journalists who drank there.

Other drinkers sat huddled in armchairs near

the warmth of the fireplace, the smoke from their cigars curling toward the flames. Some were reading from newspapers and magazines, while one bearded gentleman was penning a letter on some paper that was stretched upon his knee.

"The idea that this country's leading authors have all been hypnotized with venom extracted from an exotic spider, that the tales they are now publishing give glimpses of the future and send everybody who reads them insane." Barrett rolled his eyes. "It's beyond belief."

"But you've got to—"

Alfie tried to interrupt, but Barrett silenced him with a sharp look as he carried on speaking.

"And now you tell me that the person who is behind this sinister scheme is the recently deceased Lady Isabella Cambridge—a woman who has miraculously risen from the grave to spread chaos through the city." He laughed mirthlessly. "If you think I can get my editor to publish this nonsense, then you're the maddest of them all."

Raising his hand, Barrett called out for another drink. At the bar, the portly landlord nodded in acknowledgment, his eyes glancing up from the magazine open on the counter in front of him.

"You've got to publish this," Penelope replied, indignation rising in her voice as the buzz of conversation around them quieted. "It's the truth."

Draining the last of the beer from his glass, the

journalist shook his head dismissively as he wiped the froth from his moustache.

"I'm sorry, Miss Tredwell, or should I say Miss *Flinch*," he replied wearily, "but newspapers don't print the truth—not without proof." He banged his glass back on the table. "So, why don't you both go and bother somebody else with your childish stories and leave me alone to welcome in the new year in peace."

As he spoke these words, the pub fell silent. Turning uneasily in their chairs, Penelope and Alfie glanced around the crowded bar. At the long tables, the rattle of glasses and the low murmur of conversation had died away entirely. The drinkers gathered there sat hunched noiselessly over the tables, their inky fingers tracing the shapes of words amid the spilled drinks.

From the direction of the fireplace came the scratching sound of pen against paper. Penelope shivered in recognition. Turning, she saw the gentlemen sitting in their armchairs, slumped around the fire. Their glazed eyes reflected the orange glow of the flames and, at first glance, they merely looked as though they had drunk more than they could hold. But then Penelope saw the pens in their hands scrawling across pages of newsprint and sheets of paper.

In the armchair nearest the fire, a gentleman in a red velvet waistcoat shivered as though in the throes of a terrible nightmare, pages tumbling from his lap and falling into the flames. At his feet lay a discarded copy of the *Pall Mall Magazine*, its headline reading *Visions of the Future* hinting at the dreams that were troubling his mind.

Barrett slowly rose to his feet, his face creased in confusion. He looked around the pub in consternation as the scratching of pens grew louder. The journalist shook his head to try and clear the fug of ale from his brain.

He glanced toward the bar, but even there, the landlord was stooped over the counter, frantically scribbling. The entire pub was caught in a trance. Barrett turned toward Penelope and Alfie as they rose from their chairs, his eyes filled with horror.

"What's going on here?" he cried.

"This is your proof," Penelope replied. "I told you, the madness is spreading. Look around—see what they were reading."

Barrett glanced around the room again. He shuddered as he watched the silent rows of drinkers hunched over the tables, the constant movement of their hands scratching out endless messages. But scattered among them, he noticed for the first time the pages torn from magazines, beer-stained editions of the *Strand*, *Longman's* magazine and the *Idler*. He turned back toward Penelope.

"Make them stop," he pleaded.

Penelope looked up to meet his gaze, her pale green eyes filled with misery.

"I can't," she replied. "Once they've read the

stories, the madness is in them. Nothing can stop them from scribbling their nightmares across the page. Soon all of London is going to be a great Bedlam—the only people left sane will be locked inside the asylums."

She fell silent for a moment. The only sound they could hear was the scratching of pens and the scrape of fingernails across the wooden tables.

"I don't understand," Barrett stammered. "How can a story send you insane?"

Penelope gestured around the room at the figures slumped in armchairs and sat bent over tables, their eyes glazed and unfocused.

"The madness inside these people is just a reflection," she told him, "a hypnotic shadow cast by the stories they've read. Lady Cambridge has enslaved the minds of the greatest writers in Britain. With the venom of the dream-weaver spider flowing through their veins, their words have the power to take control of every mind in the city. We need to find a way to free them from this nightmare she has trapped them in."

Alfie frowned. "But we've already tried that," he said. "Apart from H. G. Wells, we couldn't get close to any of the authors. Every magazine in London has bolted its doors. How can we get to them?"

A cold shiver of fear crept up Penelope's spine as the answer crawled into her mind. She remembered the darkness crowding in on all sides as the venom flowed through her veins. She knew what she had to do.

"I need to drink the venom of the dream-weaver spider," she told them, unable to hide the tremor in her voice. "I have to find them in their dreams."

"What are you talking about?" Barrett asked, scratching his head in despair.

"When Lady Cambridge poisoned the authors, the spider venom took them into the heart of the madness," Penelope explained. "They've been sleepwalking through the hurly-burly of everyday life, but their minds are somewhere else as the strange visions they dream send the city insane. The venom will help me to find them."

Alfie stared at her in horror.

"But won't it send you mad as well?"

"I don't know," Penelope replied, trying to hold her voice steady as she remembered the spiders scurrying inside her mind, "but it's the only chance we have left. If I can find the authors and wake them from their dreams, then their stories will just become fantasies again. Lady Cambridge's prophecy will crumble to dust as the city is set free from her madness."

She stared up at them both, her pale green eyes glinting with a grim determination.

"I've got to try."

The journalist's moustache twitched, his instinct for a front-page story finally taking hold, but a frown stayed fixed to Alfie's face.

"The last of the venom was destroyed in the fire at Lady Cambridge's mansion," he said. "Where are you going to find an almost extinct African spider in the middle of London?"

Penelope's face crumpled in frustration. Without the spider venom, there was no way she could stop this. In a few hours' time, the secrets of the new century would belong to Lady Cambridge and the whole world would be at her mercy.

"There must be a way we can find the spider," Penelope murmured, reaching up to brush her hair from her eyes. "If we could just..."

Her voice trailed away as the hopelessness of their mission struck home. She glanced around the bar in despair as the hunched figures kept on writing, the scrape and scratch of their silent words filling her mind with misery. On the wall directly in front of her, the framed front page of a newspaper stared back. Penelope's distracted gaze slowly focused on its headline proclaiming the opening of a grand new museum. Her eyes narrowed, then her face suddenly lit up with a flash of inspiration.

"There's one place in London that might have that spider," she exclaimed. "The British Museum of Natural History!"

XXIV

"This is most irregular, Mr. Barrett."

Dressed in a shabby tweed suit, the gray-bearded curator selected a key from the bunch that dangled from his pocket chain. They had reached the end of a long corridor, tucked away in the bowels of the museum. Directly in front of them was a dark mahogany door, its sign almost lost under a layer of dust: DRY STOREROOM NO. 2. Fitting the key to the lock, he turned the handle and then pushed the door open. The curator paused on its threshold, glancing back at them with an anxious expression fixed to his face.

"If the museum's board of trustees knew that I had let you in here tonight," he said, keeping his voice low as if afraid of being overheard, "my position as curator, indeed my career as a natural historian, could be in ruins."

Penelope and Alfie shifted uncomfortably under

his gaze, but the young journalist just rested his hand on the older man's shoulder.

"I think that's the least of your worries, Mr. Wallace," Barrett told him, his tone a mixture of sympathy and menace. "I think the board of trustees would be much more interested in hearing about how that shipment of missing dinosaur bones ended up being delivered to Battersea Dogs Home. I can imagine the headlines now."

The color drained from the curator's face. "You wouldn't print that," he moaned despairingly. "You promised me!"

"Of course not," Barrett soothed. "Anybody could make a mistake like that. Don't worry, your secret's safe with me. We just need to see that spider I told you about."

Glancing nervously over his shoulder, Wallace slowly nodded his head and motioned for them to follow. He stepped into the darkened room, pulling on a light cord. With a conceited grin on his face, Barrett hurried forward to follow him, Penelope and Alfie close behind.

The huge square room looked like a museum in miniature, its walls lined with glass display cases filled with collections of desiccated specimens. Stuffed crocodiles, the shells of giant tortoises, yellowing jars of pickled scorpions and snakes, galleries of beetles and bugs, dried and displayed on a pin. Under the glimmering lamps that hung from the ceiling, long rows of mahogany tables were covered with yet more bottles and jars filled with the eerie forms of other animals: spiders, scorpions, and crabs. Stacks of wooden crates sat, unpacked, at the ends of these rows, and, in the shadows, the shapes of strange skeletons, their bones arranged into frightening poses. She shivered. A cornucopia of life preserved forever in death.

The curator hurried toward a long workbench in the center of the room. Among the jars and fume-filled bottles arranged there sat a tank of scurrying spiders. At the sight of this, a cold shiver crawled down Penelope's spine. She remembered the huge spidertorium hidden behind the bookshelves in Lady Cambridge's sitting room and her courage retreated at the thought of what she had come here to do.

As the curator delved among the exhibits, Alfie glanced across at Penelope, his face creased in concern.

"Are you sure you want to do this?" he asked.

Penelope nodded. She set her own features into a determined expression even though her mind was crawling with fear.

"It's the only way."

Wallace turned back to face them. In his hands, he held a small glass jar filled with a sickly yellow solution. Penelope could see the shape of a large spider inside the jar. Its bulbous black abdomen hung suspended in the preservative liquid as its long legs swirled in the yellowing brine. As the curator set the jar on the bench in front of them and began to unscrew the lid, Penelope glimpsed the silver crescent shape marking the spider's back. She quickly covered her mouth as a nauseating stench rose up from the jar.

"*Architarbi somnerus*," Wallace began, his voice suddenly loud in the dusty storeroom as though he was addressing a lecture hall rather than just the three of them gathered around the workbench. He slid the spider from the jar onto a metal tray. "The dream-weaver spider. As you can see," the curator continued, picking up a scalpel from the bench and pointing at the spider's body, which was oozing stickily on the tray, "it got its name from these striking moon-shaped markings. Native to a remote part of British East Africa, it was apparently prized by the natives there as a delicacy, so much so that the creature is now sadly extinct."

Penelope frowned. If only the spider had really become extinct and prevented Lady Cambridge from making her momentous discovery.

Glancing up, Wallace eyed them suspiciously.

"Why do you want to look at it anyway?" he asked. "What's so important about this spider?"

"Just a story I'm working on," Barrett replied guardedly. "Nothing important."

The curator raised a skeptical eyebrow.

"At eleven o'clock at night on New Year's Eve?"

Barrett glared back at him.

"That's right," he answered sharply. "Now, unless you want to read about how the stray dogs of Battersea have been feasting on dinosaur bones in the next edition of the *Pall Mall Gazette*, I suggest you give me some privacy to complete my research."

His face swiftly reddening, the chastened curator beat a hasty retreat. "I've got better things to do than stay here," he muttered angrily. "Lock the door on your way out."

As the storeroom door slammed shut behind him, Penelope turned toward Alfie.

"Go and keep an eye on him," she said. "Make sure he stays away."

Alfie looked at Penelope with worried eyes.

"Will you be all right?"

"I'll be fine," she replied. Beneath her dark hair, Penelope's face was already pale at the thought of what was to come. "I know what I'm doing."

Alfie frowned. There was a heartbeat of silence and then he nodded his head. As he turned to leave, he called out to Barrett, who was tentatively poking the spider's body with a pair of tweezers.

"Make sure you take care of her," he warned him. "Or else you'll have me to answer to."

Alfie's lanky figure disappeared through the door, leaving Barrett and Penelope alone in the eerie gloom of the storeroom. Penelope turned back toward the workbench.

"Right," she said, "let's get started." She held out

her hand for the tweezers and Barrett reluctantly placed them in her palm. He stared down at the black-and-silver spider, a widening circle of amber liquid spreading across the tray beneath it.

"How are we going to get the venom out of this thing?"

With the tweezers in one hand and a scalpel in the other, Penelope swiftly removed the spider's abdomen, cutting away the legs with a series of precise incisions. Using the tweezers, she carefully lifted the head that remained onto a glass slide resting beside a microscope and slid this into focus beneath the lens. As she pressed her eye to the microscope, she answered the journalist in a calm and level voice.

"I'm going to dissect the venom glands."

Openmouthed, Barrett stared at Penelope in disbelief, watching as, wielding the scalpel with her right hand, she delicately inserted the tip of a glass pipette into the spider's head with her left. Gently squeezing and then releasing the rubber bulb at the top of the pipette, tiny droplets of cloudy liquid were drawn up inside the glass tube.

"How did you learn how to do that?" he murmured.

Penelope raised her head from the microscope as though she had just completed a classroom experiment.

"I've always been interested in science," she replied.

Lifting the pipette to the light, she stared at the liquid collected inside. The glass tube was only half full, the pearly solution swirling with a nebulous glow. Penelope glanced across at Barrett, a worried look etched on her face.

"The preserving fluid has contaminated most of the venom glands," she said. "I don't know if this is enough."

Frowning, Barrett let out a long sigh.

"There's only one way to find out."

As he spoke, Penelope felt a prickle of fear run up her spine. The memory of the venom pumping through her veins crawled back into her brain. Penelope remembered the spiders scurrying inside her mind, the silken threads of their webs dragging her to the very edge of madness. She couldn't go through it again. It was too much to ask.

Then she thought of Monty and Mr. Wigram, H. G. Wells and the long rows of silent authors, all entranced by Lady Cambridge. Penelope recalled the alarming sights she had seen that day as they had wandered the city. Writing daubed on abandoned carriages and along the sides of empty houses, strange cryptic messages that made no sense at all. The passers-by sleepwalking through their lives, eyes glazed as they stared at a world that shouldn't exist. Not yet.

If she couldn't do this, then Lady Cambridge would win. She would control them all and the future would be hers. This was their only chance to fight back. She had to plunge into the heart of the madness and wake the authors from their nightmares. With her heart thudding in her chest, Penelope nodded.

"Let's do it."

Carefully handing the pipette to Barrett, Penelope seated herself on a chair beside the workbench. Clearing a space on the desk, she pulled out a pen and sheaf of paper from her handbag and placed these in front of her.

"We need to do this properly."

Inside her mind, she was screaming, but Penelope fought to keep the emotion from her face. With the pipette held between his fingers, Barrett stood over her. He looked down, his eyes darting anxiously from Penelope to the shimmering liquid captured in the pipette's glass tube.

"Are you ready?" he asked.

Penelope's fingers whitened as she gripped the arms of the chair. Taking a deep breath, she could only bring herself to whisper a single word in reply.

"Yes."

Tilting her head back, Penelope's long black hair fell from her face. She slowly opened her mouth, fighting against every instinct in her body that wanted to keep her lips firmly closed. Leaning over her, Barrett squeezed the pipette. The venom fell onto Penelope's tongue like tiny teardrops, the acrid liquid burning as it slipped down her throat.

Stepping back, Barrett watched aghast as

Penelope gagged, her slender body racked with fierce shudders as the venom worked its way through her veins. Her fingers clawed at her throat, desperately trying to free herself from the onrushing darkness. Then Penelope's hands suddenly dropped to her side, her green eyes frozen into an unsettling blank stare.

"Penny!" Barrett reached toward her in alarm. "Are you all right?"

But no answer came in reply as Penelope stared sightlessly ahead. Her gaze seemed fixed on the glass tank at the end of the workbench. Behind the glass, countless spiders scurried and crawled, their intricate silken webs echoing those spinning inside Penelope's own mind.

XXV

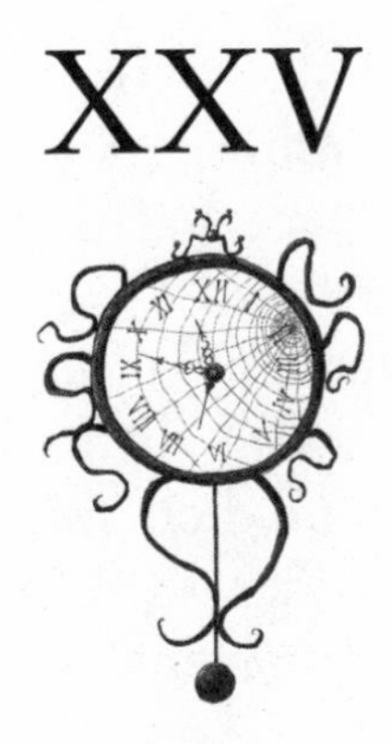

As the spiders' frenzied spinning reached a crescendo, Penelope felt herself falling into the heart of the darkness that filled her mind. And then the dreams began.

A blizzard of images flashed before her eyes like a speeded-up stereoscope, almost too swiftly at first for her to make sense of. A towering airship exploding in a ball of fire...mechanical beasts rampaging across a battlefield...a sleek arrow of steel darting across the sky...smokeless factories run by machines...babies born from test tubes...

Penelope sobbed as black silken threads wrapped themselves more tightly around her, dragging her down; her reason crumbling under the weight of the history to come. The past, present, and future didn't exist any more—everything was now. She saw great cities of glass and steel soaring into the sky and then exploding into ruins as bombs rained down before slowly rising again...a roaring procession of automobiles racing down an endless highway...her own face staring out from a mirror, impossibly old...

Penelope felt herself falling again, tumbling through the darkness. A deafening cacophony of voices echoed around her, their frenzied shouts and screams filling her ears. Millions of minds caught in a huge spiderweb of black silken threads that stretched across the city.

As the dream-weaver spiders crawled inside her mind, Penelope could see the glittering darkness at the heart of their web. She felt herself dragged toward it, the sticky threads wrapping themselves around her limbs. She glimpsed the shadowy shapes of shrouded figures waiting for her there, each and every one writhing in torment.

As she fell, a dizzying kaleidoscope of images burned through her brain. Fireworks exploding across the sky...tiny machines filled with the sounds of a thousand symphonies...a sinister man with a toothbrush moustache facing a vast crowd of people, their arms held aloft in salute...great walls of ice collapsing into the sea...earthquakes and tsunamis...gleaming shops...mechanical hearts... the crying face of a starving child...

Penelope couldn't just see the images—she was inside them. Every person, every place, every single moment: she was there.

She tumbled down into the heart of the web,

its threads shivering with delight as she landed, sprawling, in the tangled jungle of darkness. Rising to her feet, Penelope looked out into the shimmering void. The shrouded shapes of silken cocoons surrounded her, their forms twisting and writhing in the shadows. Straining her eyes, she saw a skein of silken threads emerging from the top of each cocoon, spinning upward into the darkness. Each thread pulsed with a spiraling torrent of images, ensnaring the fragile minds of the city above them. From every corner of the sky, she could hear the low moan of their voices, driven slowly insane. The web connected them all: millions of minds brought together as one. A single mind, as vast as the city itself.

As she stood there, frozen in wonder, the sticky strands of the web wrapped themselves around her limbs. She tried to tear herself free, but the dream-weaver spiders kept spinning their threads ever tighter. Penelope cried out in despair. The tangled threads of the web shivered as her voice echoed into the darkness. All around her a tumult of voices rose up in reply, drowning out her cry completely.

She tried to block out the whirl of whimpered words and snapshot images, a demented clamor that was driving her to the edge of madness. But there was no way out.

In the gloom of the museum's storeroom, Penelope's fingers twitched, grasping hold of the pen as she began to scratch a torrent of words across the paper. Barrett watched in amazement as Penelope scrawled across the empty page, his eyes widening as he read what she was writing.

Lost in the heart of the web, all should have been lost, but as the silken shroud enveloped Penelope completely, the distant feeling of the pen in her fingers felt strangely familiar. Somewhere in the farthest reaches of her mind, Penelope remembered who she was. She was a writer. An author. That was why she was here—to bring meaning to this terrifying mystery.

As the skirring whirl of images threatened to blind her—hoverships and flying liners...miniskirts... living skeletons...electrified guitars—a growing fury flushed the madness from her veins. She wasn't some helpless bystander caught up in Lady Cambridge's scheme; she was going to be the writer of this tale. And she was going to end it now.

Penelope tore her way free from the shroud, its silken threads hanging limply from her fingers. The tremors rippled through the web and a whisper of voices rose in the darkness. Pulling her legs free from the sticky threads that still clung to her, Penelope felt the spiders inside her mind scurry in fear. She turned toward the twisting shapes of the silken cocoons rising up in the darkness. With a sudden rush of realization, she knew who was trapped inside these shrouded tombs.

Scrambling across the web, Penelope reached the first of the cocoons. Her hands sunk into its sticky morass of threads. As the writhing form inside the shroud shuddered in response, she tore at the tendrils of silk, the threads snapping as her hands clawed their way free. The trailing webs tried to wrap themselves around her, but with a howl of defiance, she ripped the heart of the cocoon open, dragging the shrouded figure out of the darkness.

The freed man slumped at her feet, sticky webs still clinging to his face. Sinking to her knees, Penelope peeled the snarled threads from his whiskers. Her heart rose in her mouth as she saw the semiconscious features of Arthur Conan Doyle staring back at her. Doyle's eyes slowly flickered open as though waking from a dream. He looked up into her eyes with an awestruck gaze.

"We're so small," he breathed, his voice a cracked whisper. "We reach so high, but we fall so far. I've seen behind the veil. Everything we've dreamed will be dust by the time we are gone."

A glazed look began to descend over Doyle's eyes again, the spiders still at work inside his mind. Penelope brought her hand back and slapped him across the face. The effect was instantaneous. Doyle's eyes opened wide in indignation, his hand reaching toward his stinging cheek.

"What are you doing, girl!" he roared. "Have you gone mad?"

Doyle's anger died as swiftly as it had come

as he caught sight of the shimmering darkness surrounding them. He could see the bewildering maze of webs stretching in every direction, their gleaming threads pulsing with light, and, even closer, the grove of mummified cocoons, the shrouded shapes inside still writhing in madness.

The author glanced back fearfully at the tattered cocoon that Penelope had torn him from, its silken strands hanging in shreds.

"My God," he murmured. "It wasn't a dream."

Reaching out her hand, Penelope helped Doyle to his feet. His frightened eyes looked down into hers, his face transfixed in wonder and dread.

"What manner of place is this?" he asked her. "Where are we?"

"Inside our minds," Penelope replied. "At least, that's where I think we are." She gestured up at the countless threads of the glistening web. The darkness throbbed with a clamoring maelstrom of voices. "We're inside the minds of every soul in London who's fallen under the spell of the stories you've written."

Openmouthed, Doyle stared at her in disbelief.

"How can that be possible?"

Penelope shook her head.

"I don't have time to explain." She gestured at the dark shapes of the cocoons. "Help me get the others free."

Stifling a shiver, Doyle nodded and the two of them scrambled across the web. As they slashed and tore at the shrouds, the webbed cocoons grudgingly spewed out their captives. H. G. Wells and H. Rider Haggard, Rudyard Kipling, Max Pemberton; every author, editor, and publisher whom Penelope had seen entranced by Lady Cambridge, was soon crouched shivering in the shadows as they pulled the clinging webs from their skin.

Penelope's guardian, Mr. Wigram, raised a watery smile as she pulled the silken threads from his pale, timeworn face.

"Still researching your new story, Penelope," he murmured.

Penelope nodded, a relieved smile breaking across her own face. Beside them, Conan Doyle tore open the last of the cocoons. As its silken webs hung free, the broad-shouldered body of a man slowly slid to the floor. His hands reached up to his face, clawing at the clinging cobweb mask. As it came away with a tearing sound, Penelope saw Monty's ruddy face, his bloodshot eyes blinking in surprise.

"I feel quite ill," he wheezed.

XXVI

"But I don't understand what you're telling us." Rudyard Kipling scratched at his thinning hair as he stared up at Penelope over the frames of his silver-rimmed glasses. His face was creased in bewilderment. "You're saying that we're trapped here?"

Penelope shook her head, trying to keep an assured air as the assembled authors looked up to her for salvation. The empty husks of the cocoons around them swayed with low moans, their tiny oasis surrounded by the glistening darkness of the web.

"It's the venom that's been keeping you trapped here," she replied. "When Lady Cambridge poisoned you, she took control of your minds. The things that you've seen, the stories that you've written—it's all been for her. She's the one who has stolen your imaginations."

"That damned woman!"

Penelope flinched as the stout figure of H. Rider Haggard rose to his feet. Beneath his bristling eyebrows, his dark eyes glowered with a look that was as black as his beard.

"If what you've told us is true, this so-called lady has used us all like a bunch of ha'penny hacks! If I have my bullwhip when I finally get to meet her, I've a good mind to—"

Conan Doyle held up his hand to calm him.

"My dear Henry, I hardly think that will help us in our current predicament," he remarked dryly. Doyle turned toward Penelope, fixing her with an inquiring gaze that brought to mind his creation, the great detective, Sherlock Holmes. "What do you suggest that we do, Miss Tredwell? How do we get out of here?"

Penelope paled beneath his gaze. The wave of determination that had brought her to this point came crashing down onto an empty shore. She could see Monty, Mr. Wigram, the faces of every person there turned toward her in hope. Her mind blank of solutions as she slowly shook her head.

"I don't know," Penelope finally stammered, a blush rising to her cheeks. "I thought that if I freed you then the madness would stop." She paused and glanced up into the void; flickering images spinning across the latticework of webs as the darkness throbbed with a pandemonium of voices. "I was wrong."

Monty wailed in despair.

"I want to go home!" he cried. "This is all just a terrible nightmare." Monty grabbed hold of the flesh on his forearm and pinched himself hard then wailed again in pain. "Why can't I just wake up?"

At Monty's words, a faint glimmer of hope crept into Penelope's eyes. She looked up again into the darkness, the shimmering web trembling with a million dreams of madness. That was what was keeping them here—the countless minds locked together, trapped, mesmerized, inside their own private hell. It wasn't just the authors who she needed to wake...

"I've got it!" she cried, her eyes flashing with excitement. As the authors glanced up in surprise, Penelope flung her arms skyward. "Listen to their voices. It's your stories that have sent them into madness, but you can save them as well. You've got to write the way out. Not just for yourself, but for everyone."

They stared back at her blankly. Scratching at his thick moustache, Wells was the first to ask the question they all wanted to know.

"How?"

"You tell them a new story," Penelope explained. "A story that will help them to make sense of all this and finally wake them from their madness. At the moment, the visions they have seen are a cage trapping their dreams. Why try to escape when the future is already decided? You need to break down the bars—let them know that their lives still matter. Make them see that nothing is impossible."

There was a moment of silence and then a single voice spoke out in reply.

"I suppose it's not beyond the realms of reason," Doyle began.

Wells nodded in agreement.

"A mass hallucination, perhaps..."

"The Machiavellian scheme of a sinister society," Haggard continued, his eyes glinting as inspiration struck.

"Every living soul in the city rising up to fight back—"

The authors' voices grew louder as the frenzy of ideas took hold. Watching them, Penelope stepped forward, her own eyes shining with the spark of invention.

"Don't just talk about it," she cried. "We need to write our stories straight into their minds."

Penelope raced to the nearest cocoon, its crown still spinning out a spiral of threads into the darkness. She grasped hold of the trailing strands, wrapping the glistening cords around her fingers. Glancing back over her shoulder, Penelope shouted her instructions to the rest.

"Get to work," she ordered them. "Wake the sleeping city. Set them free."

Rousing themselves from their conference, the authors hurried to the empty shrouds. As they lashed themselves to the cocoons, willingly wrapping the silken threads against their skin, the web started to pulse with a new light. The flickering spiral of images glowed with strange hues, their brightness almost blinding amid the darkness.

Penelope could feel the minds of the city above turning toward them, desperate for the freedom they had gained. Tightening her grip on the silken strands in her hands, Penelope shook the web with all her might.

You're not sleeping, she told them, her voice ringing across the darkness. *You're not dreaming. You are alive.*

The words came back to her in an echoing reply.

We're not sleeping. We're not dreaming. We are alive.

This doesn't have to be your future. Penelope screamed into the void. *Fight back. The future is yours to write.*

As the threads of the web hung free, the clamor of voices in the darkness rose to an answering crescendo.

Fight back. Fight back. Fight back.

The huge spiderweb shook, its glistening threads straining as the authors spun their tales. Penelope gripped the silken strands of the cocoon more tightly, her eyes blazing with imagination's unquenchable fire. From every tattered shroud shone a brilliant skein of threads, lighting a path through the darkness of their minds and setting the dreamers free.

Great tremors tore at the web. From every corner of its vast latticework there came a hideous creaking, the spiraling threads flailing wildly as they snapped. A deafening cacophony of voices filled Penelope's mind, their cries now charged with joy. With a sudden wrenching sound, the shimmering web collapsed into the darkness of the abyss. The clamor of voices suddenly snapped into silence as, out across the city, the sleepers began to wake.

In the shadow of Big Ben, a bedraggled tramp rose from the gutter, rubbing the mists from his eyes. He shrugged a tattered blanket of newsprint from his shoulders as he gazed up at the clock, its large hand pointing twelve minutes to midnight. Beyond the clock tower, he could see a glittering sea of stars filling the sky.

"I had the most remarkable dream," he murmured.

As the pen fell from Penelope's fingers, Barrett finished reading the last sentence she had written. He sat there in a stunned silence, his brow furrowed in thought.

Everything that Penelope had told him, from the madness spreading across the city to the fact that she was Montgomery Flinch, was true. He stared down at the stack of papers by Penelope's side as she began to stir from her sleep. Here was his proof—the pages filled with Penelope's elegant handwriting setting down every twist in the tale and telling of the world yet to come. It was the story of a lifetime—a guaranteed front-page sensation. Forget about the *Pall Mall Gazette*, he could take this to the *Morning Herald*, the *Times* even.

The journalist eased the papers from beneath Penelope's hand, gathering them up into his arms as he turned to leave.

"I'm sorry," he muttered as Penelope's eyelashes began to flicker. "But I can't miss out on a scoop like this."

Barrett scurried toward the door, skirting the shadowy margins of the storeroom in his hurry to leave. As he reached up to brush a hanging cobweb from his path, a large brown spider fell onto his face. Stumbling back in fear, Barrett screamed as the spider's fangs sunk into his skin, color quickly draining from his face as the venom pumped through his veins. The journalist clutched at his chest, the papers scattering to the floor as his mouth contorted in a rictus of pain. He staggered forward, then toppled and fell, his body lying motionless by the feet of a stuffed panda.

A dark figure stepped from the shadows, her long black coat fastened to her chin. She stooped to collect the fallen papers, smiling as she glanced down at the pages, and then stepped toward Penelope as she slowly stirred from her sleep.

Leaning over her, she gently brushed her hand

across Penelope's cheek as her pale green eyes flickered open.

"Wake up, deary," Lady Cambridge purred. "It's nearly midnight."

XXVII

Trying to shake the sleep from her bones, Penelope pulled herself upright. Her heart thudded in her chest as she saw Lady Cambridge standing in front of her, a nightmare come to life. In her right hand she held a small pistol, its sleek black barrel pointing straight at Penelope. A mocking smile played across Lady Cambridge's lips.

"I'm so glad you could join me," she said. "The new century approaches—my finest hour is at hand."

"You've failed," Penelope retorted. "All across the city the people are waking up. The madness is gone."

Her smile widening, Lady Cambridge shook her head.

"I'm afraid you're quite mistaken," she replied in a triumphant tone. "The madness is yet to come. We stand on the brink of a century of insanity—all reason lost as the world tumbles toward wars, famines, plagues, and disasters. And with these" —in her left hand, she brandished the pages Penelope had written—"I have the map to chart a course through the madness—available, of course, to the highest bidder."

She glanced down at the papers again, her icy blue eyes narrowing in delight.

"I must congratulate you, my dear," Lady Cambridge continued. "I thought the other writers were good, but you make the future read like poetry. If I had realized sooner that you were really Montgomery Flinch, then I'd have kept you chained in my cellar writing the history of the world still to come."

Penelope shivered. Rising to her feet, she eyed the pistol nervously as she began to back away. Her right hand trailed against the edge of the workbench, trying to find some kind of weapon she could use to protect herself. Lady Cambridge watched her, her eyes twinkling in amusement.

"There's no way out," she gently scolded. "This is my father's museum; I spent my childhood here studying these beautiful creatures and learning their secrets. You should have remembered what the spider does when its web is destroyed. It spins a new one—even grander and more beautiful than the last. You are at the heart of my web, Miss Tredwell, and soon it will cover the entire world."

She advanced toward Penelope; a smiling huntress stalking her prey.

Still backing away as she reached the end of the aisle, Penelope stumbled over something lying half-hidden in the shadow cast by a towering stack of crates. She glanced down to see Barrett's sightless eyes staring back at her, a large brown spider crawling hungrily across his face.

"You've killed him," she gasped.

Lady Cambridge frowned. "The funnel-weaver spider isn't deadly," she replied sharply. "Apart from a mild case of paralysis, temporary blindness, and irreversible memory loss, most of its victims soon recover in a matter of minutes."

She took another step toward Penelope, shortening the distance between them to a matter of feet.

"But I will be long gone by then," she continued. Lady Cambridge raised the pistol and pointed it straight at Penelope's head. "And so will you."

As she stared down the barrel, Penelope saw a flurry of images flash before her eyes. Not memories of her own life, but images of the world yet to come—airplanes, rocket ships, skyscrapers, and laser beams—countless wonders she would never live to see if the bullet found its target.

As the pistol was cocked, the click of its hammer sounded like a cannon and Penelope threw herself behind the crates stacked at the end of the desk. The wooden cases toppled forward and then a shot rang out, the bullet splintering the falling crates as they crashed down onto Lady Cambridge. She let out a terrified yell, the crushing weight of the boxes sending her sprawling.

As Penelope peered around the edge of the desk, she saw Lady Cambridge pinned beneath the shattered remains of a heavy packing case.

"Help me," she called out, raising her hand pitifully, as the contents of the case crawled free. Penelope glimpsed the grimy label fixed to the lid of the broken crate.

BRITISH EMPIRE AFRICAN EXPEDITION
BOX No. 5
For the attention of Professor Stebbing, Arachnology Department
ARCHITARBI INCUBUS
HANDLE WITH CARE

The large black spiders scuttled inquisitively toward Lady Cambridge, her pale face frozen in fear. She struggled to free herself, but the crushing weight of the shattered case held her captive. A low moan escaped from her lips as the largest of the spiders began to crawl across her face. Penelope could see the silvery mark on its back, the shape of a circle like a full moon. For a moment, her eyes met Lady Cambridge's and she saw the fear and hatred burning there. Then the spider struck.

Lady Cambridge let out a banshee wail and Penelope turned away in revulsion. She sank to her knees next to Barrett's prone body, his blank eyes still staring out into oblivion as if he were dead. Penelope pressed her fingers to his neck, desperately searching for a pulse. She felt a distant throbbing beneath her fingers as Barrett's heart pumped the venom from his veins.

The storeroom door burst open and Alfie stood framed in the doorway, flanked by the two stuffed grizzly bears standing sentry there. Seeing Penelope kneeling over the journalist, he raced to her side.

"Are you all right?"

Alfie's expression quickly turned to horror as he glanced past Penelope and saw the black tide of bugs inching out of the wreckage and across Lady Cambridge's trapped body. Her face was almost completely hidden by the spiders crawling over her skin. "What happened here?" he murmured. "Is that Lady Cambridge?"

Penelope nodded, a haunted look in her eyes. "She got a taste of her own medicine."

Between them, Barrett began to stir and the two of them glanced down to see the journalist's eyes slowly swim into focus.

"Mr. Barrett, are you all right?" Penelope bent her head closer to hear the soft whisper of his reply. "Don't worry, it's over now."

Barrett stared up at her, his brow creased in confusion.

"Who are you?" he asked.

XXVIII

Monty held a cold flannel to his head, his bloodshot eyes staring out into the dawn's gray light.

"It's my worst New Year's Eve hangover ever," he groaned as Alfie placed a glass of Barber's Patented Reviving Cure on the desk in front of him. Monty eyed the colorless liquid with disdain. "And I didn't even have a drink!"

At the desk beside him, Mr. Wigram shared Monty's deathly pallor, but the lawyer's haggard face creased in a frown as Monty let out another theatrical groan.

"We are all feeling the effects of last night's endeavors, Mr. Maples," he replied caustically. "Although if Penelope hadn't told us exactly what had happened, I would have believed the whole thing one of those remarkable dreams that dissolve into mist upon waking. But I kindly suggest that you manage to bear your imagined sufferings a little less noisily."

Alfie grinned as Monty bristled in indignation.

"Here's something to cheer about," he announced, quickly filling the silence before Monty had a chance to reply. Alfie plucked a rolled-up newspaper from his pocket and unfurled it on the desk in front of Penelope. "Look at page seven under News in Brief."

Beneath the newspaper banner and the dateline reading *Monday, 1 January 1900*, the headline proclaimed in large black letters:

THE WORLD WAKES TO A NEW CENTURY

That morning, all across the city, the spellbound readers had woken too. Rubbing the sleep from their eyes, the strange visions they had seen of the world still to come had slowly faded away until only fragments remained, like some half-forgotten dream. As maids cleared the magazines from bedside tables, their stories of the new century had ended up in wastebaskets or torn into strips as kindling for the fire. The only power now left in their pages a guttering flame to ward off the winter chill.

Penelope flicked through the newspaper until she found page seven, her eyes scanning across the rows of columns before spotting the brief article at the top of the page. With a satisfied smile, she read the story aloud.

"Lady Cambridge, who had been feared dead in

the recent fire which destroyed her home, was found alive in dramatic circumstances last night. She was discovered at the British Museum of Natural History suffering from a severe bout of amnesia. Doctors believe that this condition was caused by a bite from an exotic spider. Lady Cambridge is now recuperating in a private hospital."

Alfie's grin widened.

"Yes, Bedlam," he added.

Penelope nodded. The avalanche of spider bites that had rained down on her had sent Lady Cambridge into the arms of madness. As the strange scenes at the museum had come to a close, Penelope had watched as Lady Cambridge's straitjacketed body was wheeled away by a team of white-coated orderlies, her wild-eyed ravings revealing a mind unhinged by nightmares. The cell next to her mother's was waiting for her at the asylum.

"And that journalist," Alfie asked. "He still can't remember a thing?"

"You saw for yourself," Penelope replied. "Mr. Barrett didn't know what on earth he was doing there in the museum. He couldn't remember a thing from the moment he clocked off from the *Gazette* on New Year's Eve." She let out a deep sigh of relief. "He couldn't even remember my name—let alone believe that I was Montgomery Flinch."

At this news, Monty let out his own low moan of relief.

"So my job is safe then?"

Penelope glanced up at Monty. The actor's face was set in a piteous expression, but a faint glimmer of hope shone in his eyes.

"Mr. Wigram," said Penelope, turning toward her guardian. "Could you write Monty a check for the next installment of his fee?"

Monty's mournful features dissolved into a broad smile.

"Thank you," he cried, raising his glass in salute. "I won't disappoint you."

He drained the glass in triumph but then suddenly grimaced as the bitter taste of the cure trickled down his throat.

"I know you won't," Penelope replied sternly. "This is an advance on expenses to cover a January tour of the provinces—promotion for Montgomery Flinch's first story of the twentieth century in the next edition of the *Penny Dreadful*." She reached for a fresh sheet of foolscap paper and picked up her pen. "Just as soon as I have written it."

Alfie scratched his head.

"What about that story you wrote at the museum?" he asked.

Penelope quickly shook her head, her eyes darting involuntarily to the locked drawer in her desk. There in the darkness, the stacked pages filled with her fevered handwriting were filed away—a rainy day insurance policy perhaps against writer's block.

"I must have mislaid it in all the confusion," she replied with a rueful smile. "Never mind, it's probably for the best. I think there are some things that are best left to our imaginations."